A World of Wonder

by
Paul McCusker

Augustine Institute
Greenwood Village, CO

Augustine Institute
6160 S. Syracuse Way, Suite 310
Greenwood Village, CO 80111
Tel: (866) 767-3155
www.augustineinstitute.org

Note: Different versions of some of these stories
have appeared in the *Signs of Grace* series.

Creative Director: Ben Dybas
Cover Design: Lisa Marie Patterson
Illustrations: Robert Dunn

ISBN-978-1-7335221-6-8
Library of Congress Control Number 2019933067

Printed in Canada ∞

Contents

Introduction

Nicholas and Samantha Perry are twins. Nicholas is usually called Nick and Samantha is called Sam. They are both eight years old. They live in Hope Springs in Colorado. It is a town that has a lot of fun things to do.

Nick and Sam attend the St. Clare of Assisi Catholic Church and its school. Their teacher is Sister Lucy. The twins like Sister Lucy a lot.

Father Cliff Montgomery is the pastor at St. Clare's. He is young and full of energy. Deacon Chuck Crosby is older and helps Father Cliff a lot. Norm Sullivan is the handyman for the church and the school. He is friendly and has an unusual way of thinking about things.

Nick's best friends are Brad and Riley. Brad sometimes leads Nick and Sam into trouble. Riley is interested in things like Big Foot, aliens, conspiracies, and anything weird.

Sam's best friend is Kim. Kim was born in China. She now lives in Hope Springs with her aunt and uncle.

Nick and Sam have a ten-year-old sister named Lizzy. Lizzy is short for Elizabeth. They also have a twelve-year-old brother named Andrew. Their parents are named Jon and Belle.

Nick and Sam like Hope Springs. Their father's family has lived there for over a hundred years. They're glad they left the big city of Denver to settle there.

Our stories tell about Nick's and Sam's life, adventures, and struggles in Hope Springs. Maybe their lives are a lot like yours.

— . —

CHAPTER ONE

Sisters and Snowballs

Samantha Perry stood at the large window near the kitchen table in her house. Snow had fallen overnight and covered the lawn, the patio, the little picnic table, and the handful of trees near the edge of their yard.

"When is spring coming?" Sam asked her mother.

"I'm sure it'll get here sooner or later," Sam's mom said. She was on the other side of the counter making a pot of coffee.

Sam breathed onto the glass. Then she used her finger to draw a smiley face.

Sam's brother Andrew sat at the kitchen table. He was eating a bowl of cereal. "This is Colorado. Spring usually gets here just in time for summer," he said with a smile.

This would have been a snow day, Sam thought. But the school was closed because it was Easter Monday.

Loud thumps came down the stairs. Nick, Sam's twin brother, raced into the room. "Where are my boots and gloves?" he asked.

"In the side closet where they belong," Mrs. Perry said.

Nick dashed through the kitchen to the small room that had the closet where they kept their hats and coats. Sam could hear Nick banging around.

"Where do you think you're going?" Mrs. Perry called after him.

"I'm going to meet Brad and Riley

and a few other kids at the school playground," Nick shouted. "It's a good day for snowball battles."

"You're going to the school when you don't have to?" Andrew called out.

Nick appeared in the doorway with his coat on. "It's not like I'm going to class," Nick said to him. He looked up at his mother. "Is it okay?"

"You're standing there dressed to go out, and *then* you ask?" Mrs. Perry asked.

"Please?" Nick begged.

Mrs. Perry nodded. "Go on. But don't throw any snowballs at any buildings or—"

"Cars," Nick added.

"Or people walking by," added Andrew.

"Or small children," Sam said last.

The kids knew the rules well.

"May I go?" Sam asked.

"If you want," Mrs. Perry said.

Sam would call her best friend Kim to see if she wanted to go, too.

Sam wore a heavy pink coat. She wore thick gloves and her favorite black boots that went up to her knees.

The tops of branches, fences, poles, signs, and cars were lined with a thick white cover. The lawns were untouched by footprints. A few people were out shoveling their driveways. The roads had rows of tire marks on them.

It was a ten-minute walk to the school. Nick and Sam turned left here and right there before they reached the main road. They found the crosswalk and looked both ways. Sam grabbed Nick's hand as they crossed. It was an old habit.

St. Clare's Catholic School was just ahead. Laughter and shouting came from the schoolyard.

"Who is that?" Nick asked.

Sam and Nick rounded the corner. They suddenly stopped in their tracks.

In the middle of the playground,

a group of the Sisters who taught at the school were throwing snowballs at each other. One of the Sisters lay in the snow, moving her arms and legs to make a snow angel. Two of the Sisters were rolling large balls of snow to build a snowman. One of the two turned. It was Sister Lucy, their third-grade teacher. She waved at them.

St. Clare's teachers were part of an order that handled all the duties at the school. They lived in a house on the other side of the church. They all wore their long white dresses that reached down to their boots with the black veils and white bands over their hair. They had on overcoats and gloves. "I wish I could take a picture," Sam said. They reached the short wooden fence that bordered the school.

"It's weird to see nuns playing," said Nick.

Suddenly a snowball hit Nick's leg.

The twins looked up. Brad was walking toward them. Riley followed close behind him.

"They took over our playground," Brad complained.

Sam said, "They have to play *somewhere.*"

Riley looked at them with a frown. "Are nuns allowed to do that?" he asked.

"I thought they're supposed to pray all the time and look old," Brad said.

Sam's friend Kim Lee came running toward them from another direction. She pointed to the Sisters and had the same look Sam and Nick had.

"What is this?" Kim asked.

"Hey!" someone called out. It was Sister Lucy. She stomped through the snow to the fence. "Come help me build a snowman," she said. Her cheeks were red from the cold. Her eyes were bright.

"We came to have a snowball battle," Brad said.

Sister Lucy smiled. "We can do that, too. Boys against girls."

The kids looked at each other.

"It won't be fair," Brad said.

"Why not?" asked Sister Lucy.

"My parents will ground me if I hit a nun with a snowball," he said.

"Not if I hit you first," she said. She knelt and made a snowball. She stood up again. "You better run," she said to Brad.

Brad laughed, but didn't move. Then he realized she was serious. He backed away. "Let the battle begin!" he shouted as he ran off. Nick and Riley ran after him.

"Three of them and three of us," Sister Lucy said. "Come on."

Sam laughed. Kim giggled. They ran to the gate in the fence and went into the playground.

The Great Easter Monday Snow Battle—as it came to be known—lasted for over an hour and grew in size as it went. Boys from the neighborhood joined with Nick, Brad, and Riley. The Sisters rallied around the girls. The two sides squared off across the playground. Then the boys tried to invade the girls' side. Chaos followed as the boys and girls chased each other with handfuls of snowballs. They ran behind the playground equipment and around the trees.

Everything came to a sudden stop when a police car pulled up to the curb. A policeman climbed out of the car. He rounded the car and looked at them for a moment. Then he slowly walked to the battleground.

"What's going on here?" he called out.

Sister Lucy stepped up to him. "Is something wrong, officer?"

"Yes," he said. He looked at Sister with a serious expression. "I see *ten* girls and only *seven* boys."

Sister Lucy gazed at him. "What are you going to do about it?"

"I'm going to help the boys," he said. He quickly threw a snowball at her. He'd had it hidden in his gloved hand.

"Bob!" she cried out and stepped back. "That's cheating!"

The boys cheered.

The battle resumed with Bob the Policeman throwing boldly for his side.

"Are we allowed to throw snowballs at a policeman?" Sam asked Sister Lucy.

"He threw one at a nun, didn't he?" she asked.

The boys' victory didn't last very long. Bob the Policeman got a call on his radio. A stoplight wasn't working, so he was needed to direct traffic. With a friendly wave, he left.

A few minutes after that, both sides broke ranks. It was no longer boys against girls, but a free-for-all with everyone against everyone else.

At one point, Sam was side-by-side with Riley behind a snowbank. They were trying to fight off an attack from a couple of the neighborhood boys.

Sam stooped down to make snowballs. She handed them to Riley. He had better aim than she did. Then she stopped. She had a funny feeling in her stomach. *Something is wrong,* she thought.

"What are you doing?" Riley shouted.

Then, without looking, Sam stood up and shouted, "Nick! Watch out!"

Nick was throwing snowballs from under the tree near the slide. Brad was in a branch above him. Brad was about to

drop a large clump of snow on top of him.

Nick heard Sam and dove out of the way. The clump of snow hit the ground next to him.

"No fair!" Brad shouted.

"Thanks!" Nick yelled. He pelted Brad with snowballs.

Riley looked confused. "How did you do that?" he asked Sam. "You couldn't see Nick from where you were."

Sam didn't get a chance to respond. A volley of snowballs came their way, forcing them back into the battle.

Shortly after that, the Sisters called for a truce. Sister Beatrice, the kindergarten teacher, called out, "Let's go in for something hot to drink!"

The kids followed the Sisters into a side door to the school. They went to the cafeteria. Sister Stephanie, the principal, was already there with cups of steaming hot chocolate on the counter.

Some of the kids argued about who

won the battle. Some talked about their favorite moments in the battle. Some marveled at the Sisters' good aim. All of them agreed about how much fun they had.

Sam was aware that Riley kept looking at her. Then he edged over to her. "How did you know Brad was going to drop snow on Nick?"

Sam shrugged. "I don't know," she said.

She was telling the truth. That feeling in her stomach sometimes happened when Nick was in trouble. Nick once said he had the same feeling sometimes. But Sam didn't mention any of that to Riley. She thought it was none of his business.

Riley leaned close like he was sharing a secret. "Is it because you're twins?"

Sam shrugged again.

"I've heard about that," Riley said. "Twins have a kind of mind reading."

"I can't read Nick's mind," Sam said firmly.

Riley looked puzzled. "Don't be mad," he said.

"I don't want to talk about it," Sam said.

Sister Lucy stepped over to them. "What are you talking about?" she asked.

"Twins," Riley said.

"*Riley* was talking about twins," Sam said. "I wasn't."

Riley wasn't put off. "There's something strange about twins. I saw a thing about it on the internet. Scientists think twins have a special power."

"We don't have a *special power*," Sam said sharply.

"There are a lot of things we don't understand about people or the world around us," Sister Lucy said.

"Like Big Foot," Riley said.

Sam rolled her eyes. Riley often talked about Big Foot.

"The world is still full of mysteries," Sister Lucy said. "Scientists don't know how life began. They don't understand how gravity can be so weak and so strong at the same time. They can't cure cancer."

Sam was aware that Sister Lucy had slowly moved between her and Riley.

Sister Lucy said, "Science can point at things and tell us about them, but it can't answer all our questions."

"Like, if I sneeze really hard, can I make my hair stand up straight?" Riley asked. "Or blow my shoes off my feet?"

Sister Lucy laughed. "You can think about it for your science project. It's coming up."

"Science projects?" Sam asked.

Sister Lucy smiled at her. "We shouldn't talk about school work on Easter Monday. I'll tell you about it tomorrow."

Sam wandered away to find Nick. He was in the corner of the room trying to get the snow out of his ears. "I hope I don't get an earache," he said. Nick shook his head quickly like a wet dog.

"Let's go home," Sam said.

Nick knew that tone of voice. "What's wrong?" he asked.

"I'm cold and wet," she said.

Nick looked at her like he thought something else was wrong. But he didn't ask. They said their goodbyes and left.

On the way home, Nick said, "Thanks for warning me about Brad in the tree. It's a good thing you saw him."

She gave Nick a small smile. "Yeah. Good thing," she said. But she wasn't so sure. She had a feeling Riley was going to talk about it again.

CHAPTER TWO

—.—

Science and Sacrifices

The next day in class, Sister Lucy passed out papers to her students. "It's time for our science projects," she said.

Nick read the sheet on his desk. It had instructions about how to do the science project. There was also a list of science project ideas.

"You may use this list for ideas or come up with some of your own," Sister Lucy said. "But you have to decide fast because you can't do the same thing that someone else is doing. Talk to your parents. Submit your project idea to me by Friday."

Nick looked over at Sam. She was reading the sheet. He glanced up at him. She looked worried. They both remembered how much work it took to do Andrew's and Lizzy's science projects in the past.

Riley leaned forward on his desk and came into Nick's view. He looked at Nick, then Sam, then back at Nick again. He had a funny look on his face.

"What?" Nick said.

"Nothing," Riley said. He leaned back out of view again.

Nick thought, *Riley will probably do a science project about aliens.*

Later in the morning, Father Cliff Montgomery came into the class. He explained that they were all going to learn about the most important sacrament of them all.

"Everyone put on your coats," Father

Cliff said. "We're going to walk over to the old chapel."

The old chapel sat on the other side of the church property. It was small with a pointed roof and a bell tower on top. The school sometimes used the chapel for special events and as a quiet place to pray. Sometimes people got married in it.

The class followed Father Cliff inside. The floorboards creaked as they entered. The pews were made of dark wood. The windows had stained glass images of scenes from the life of Jesus. The altar was a simple table pressed against the back wall. A crucifix on a stand sat in the center. A chalice and paten sat beside it.

Sister Lucy told the class to sit in the pews. Nick scooted in next to Brad.

"What are we doing here?" Brad asked.

Nick shrugged.

Father Cliff went to the front of the chapel. "I'll tell you a story," he said.

"Years and years ago, a milkman was doing his rounds in Hope Springs. He was driving a horse and coach like he always did. As he came past the church, the horse suddenly stopped. It snorted and stomped its hooves. Something was wrong. The milkman looked around and saw smoke coming from the church. *This* church. The building was on fire."

Nick looked at the walls as if he expected to see burnt wood.

Father Cliff said, "The milkman rushed to the house next door to tell Father Bailey. Father Bailey came running with the keys to the church. He raced up the steps and opened the doors. But the flames were already so high and the fire so hot that he had to step back."

Father Cliff raised his hands and stepped back as if he could feel the fire.

"Meanwhile the milkman went to get

the fire department. A crowd gathered. Some of the people ran to get buckets of water. Others stood and watched. A few wept at the destruction of their church." Father Cliff shook his head sadly. "*Suddenly* Father Bailey dashed up the stairs again and straight into the fire!"

Some of the kids gasped.

"People were shocked," said Father Cliff. "They thought he'd gone insane. Some of them thought he'd gone in to save some valuable paintings or the gold candles on the altar. The smoke poured out. The flames reached the roof."

"Did he die?" a small voice asked. It was Kate Gallagher.

Father Cliff held up a hand for her to wait. "The firemen and the wagon arrived," he said. "They pumped water onto the burning roof. Everyone wondered about Father Bailey."

Father Cliff went to a side door. He

threw it open. Daylight and cold air flooded in. He said, "There was a loud *bang* as the side door flew open and hit the wall. Father Bailey staggered out and fell to the ground. He was covered in soot. Smoke came off of his hair and clothes. Some of the townspeople circled around him. He clutched something in his hands and held it close to his chest."

Father Cliff closed the door again. He walked up to the altar. He asked them, "What was so important that Father Bailey would run into a burning building to save it?"

"A kitten," said Rooney Conroy.

Some of the kids laughed.

Father Cliff smiled. "Father Bailey opened his hands. In one, wrapped in a cloth, was the Host. In the other, he held a small glass container with the wine in it. Father Bailey went into the fire to save the Precious Body and Blood of Jesus."

The kids shuffled in their seats.

Brad frowned at Nick.

Father Cliff waved at the chapel around them. "The chapel was burned down to the ground. We're sitting in the church they built after that."

So the old chapel is really a newer chapel, Nick thought.

Father Cliff said, "I want you to think about it. Of all the treasures he could have saved—the valuable paintings or the gold—why did Father Bailey risk his life to save some wafers and some wine from the flames?"

No one spoke.

"Some people say the bread and wine are just symbols," said Father Cliff. "If that's true, then who cares if they burn up?"

Father Cliff paced in front of the class. "That priest believed the wafer and wine were not just symbols. They were something *real*—real enough to risk his life to save them. I want you to think about that until the next time."

Sister Lucy stepped forward. "We're going to learn about the Body and Blood of Jesus so you can take your First Communion on the second Sunday in May. I'll be giving you the forms and schedule to take home to your parents," Sister Lucy said. "Make sure to note that the retreat for your First Communion is on the first Saturday in May and then the Mass for your First Communion is on Sunday a week later."

Nick knew this was a big deal. He also knew that he didn't understand how the wafer and the wine could be the Body and Blood of Jesus. His parents had tried to explain it to him once. It was confusing.

Why would a priest nearly die for a cracker and a drink? Nick wondered.

• • •

It was time for lunch after that. Nick sat with Brad and Riley.

Nick was thinking about the church fire. *That priest could have died while trying to save a wafer and some wine. Why?*

Brad was complaining about the science project. "What am I going to do?" he asked as he opened his lunch bag. "Everything on the list looks so hard."

"It's not that bad," said Riley. He was eating something that smelled like a tuna sandwich.

"Your sandwich could be a science project," Nick said. "Is that tuna?"

Riley took a bite of the sandwich and chewed. "I think so."

Nick was glad he had peanut butter and jelly.

"What are you going to do, Riley?" Brad asked. "Big Foot? The Loch Ness Monster?"

"I have an idea," said Riley.

"What idea?" asked Nick.

Riley gave him a curious look. "You'll see."

Brad dumped his lunch bag onto the table. There was a sandwich, an apple, and a yellow Twinkle Cake wrapped in plastic. Brad picked up the Twinkle Cake. It was a bright yellow sponge cake with white cream inside.

"I know what I'll do!" Brad said. "Last week I found a Twinkle Cake in the back of my closet. It was in a box for a pair of tennis shoes my mom bought last August."

"Ew," Riley said. "It was in there for almost a year?"

Brad nodded. "So my project will be to find out how long it takes a Twinkle Cake to rot in the back of a closet."

"Ew," Riley said again.

Nick thought about a sandwich he had left under his bed once. It turned blue and green on the plate.

"That'll be a *great* project," Nick said to Brad.

CHAPTER THREE

——— · ———

Faith and Impact

The Perry family talked about the science projects while they cleared the table after dinner.

Sam's dad groaned. "I hoped science projects were a Denver thing," he said. "I thought a Catholic school in Hope Springs didn't do them. That's why I moved here."

"He's joking," said Mrs. Perry. She took a pile of plates to the sink.

Lizzy looked puzzled. "Science projects aren't *that* hard, are they?" she asked.

"Let me think," Mr. Perry said. He tapped his chin with his forefinger. "There was Andrew's project with the crickets."

"Crickets?" Sam asked.

Andrew picked up a bowl and placed it on the counter. "I had to show how crickets reacted to different kinds of surroundings."

"That doesn't sound hard," Nick said.

"He spilled one of the containers. We had crickets all over the house for days," said Mrs. Perry. "I hate crickets."

Sam shuddered. "I remember now. I woke up with a cricket crawling on my face."

"And there was Lizzy's earthworm project," Mr. Perry said.

"Oh," Lizzy said with a sheepish look.

Nick carried a basket of bread to the counter. "What happened?" he asked as he took a bite out of a roll.

"I tried to show what happens to earthworms with different kinds of light," Lizzy said.

Mrs. Perry said, "She decided to use an old heat lamp I had in the closet."

"It was a bare bulb that got hot really fast," Mr. Perry chimed in.

Lizzy looked unhappy. "I turned it on the container of earthworms and then forgot about it. Those poor earthworms never had a chance."

Mr. Perry gathered up the water glasses. "But the project was a success. You learned that intense heat kills earthworms."

"It's not just the project," Mrs. Perry said. She put the last of the green beans into a plastic container. "It's the arguing and nagging and remembering to write things down and using the right display materials and getting everything done on time. It's a lot of wear and tear on everyone."

Andrew said, "Someone should do a science project about the impact of

science projects on our family."

Sam raised her hand, "I'll do that."

The family talked about the kinds of questions she would have to ask to do the project correctly.

Afterward, Nick said, "What about *me*? What am I going to do?"

Mr. Perry thought for a moment. Then he said, "I once did a project about how long it takes for nails to rust in different liquids. That one was fairly easy."

"I'll do it," Nick said.

The family continued to clear up the dishes. When they were finished, Mrs. Perry asked Nick and Sam, "Are you forgetting something?"

The twins looked at each other.

"First Communion?" Mrs. Perry reminded them.

"Oh!" Sam said. She went to her backpack and found the papers Sister Lucy had given her.

Nick ran up to his room. He came back a moment later with the same papers.

Mr. Perry looked over the forms. "This is exciting," he said.

"I still don't get it," Nick said. "How do the wafer and wine become the Body and Blood of Jesus?"

"I don't understand it either," Sam admitted.

"That's because it's hard to under-stand," Mrs. Perry said. "I don't think anyone has ever come up with a good explanation."

"Then what are we supposed to do?" Nick asked.

"You have to do what Christians have been doing from the beginning," Mr. Perry said. "You have to take it on faith."

"That's a lot of faith," said Sam.

...

Right before bedtime, Nick came into Sam's room. Sam was sitting in her bed reading a book about a girl stuck alone on a desert island.

Nick jumped onto the mattress. "I'm worried," he said.

"I know," Sam said.

"Can we take Communion if we don't know how it works?" Nick asked.

Sam thought about it. "I hope so," she said. "I don't know how light bulbs work, but I still use them. I can't drive a car, but I still ride in one. I don't know how water gets from the heater in the basement all the way up to our bathtub, but I still take baths."

Nick folded his arms. "Is that faith?" he asked.

Sam didn't know how to answer him.

CHAPTER FOUR

—.—

Slides and Cells

A couple of days later, Sister Lucy's third-grade class went to the science room in the middle school wing. The science teacher was a man named Mr. Noble who had wild white hair and big round glasses with black frames.

"Just like Albert Einstein," whispered Riley to Nick.

Part of the room had rows of desks. Another part had large counters with stools all around them. Nick saw test tubes and beakers and Bunsen burners and several microscopes.

Mr. Noble told the class to sit down at the desks. Some of the kids giggled when they did. The desks came up to the tops of their chests.

"Science has helped us to understand a lot about our world," Mr. Noble said. "It has answered many questions that mankind has asked for hundreds of years."

He paused and looked at the class.

"But there are some questions that science can't answer," he said. "Science can't tell us why we yawn or why butterflies migrate the way they do."

"They go to Mexico," Riley whispered.

Mr. Noble went on: "Science can't *prove* what we call 'reality.' Maybe you're sitting in this class right now. Or maybe you are lying in a bed somewhere sleeping. How can we *prove* that we're not in a dream?"

Nick looked around. *I wouldn't dream*

about being in a class if I had a choice,
he thought.

Riley raised his hand.

Mr. Noble pointed to him.

"I'm not in a dream because I'm
awake," Riley said. "I remember getting
out of bed."

"What if you only dreamt that you got
out of bed? What if you are dreaming
that you're awake?" Mr. Noble asked.

Riley looked like he was going to
answer, but then he slumped down in his
chair.

"Science can't *prove* love," Mr. Noble
said. "Science can't *prove* good or evil.
Science can't *prove* that there is or isn't
a God. Many questions don't fit with
science. What would you say if I asked
you, how big is the color yellow? Is it as
big as the sun or as small as the dot of
a yellow crayon?"

No one tried to answer the question.

"There are some questions we can't

answer because the questions are wrong," he said.

He paced a few steps in front of his desk. Then he picked up his phone and said, "Smile!" He took a photo of the class before anyone could react.

He picked up a small device that looked like a television remote control. He pushed a button. A screen lowered in front of the large blackboard. He touched another button, and the lights in the room dimmed. Then a bright light came on the screen. Then the photo he had just taken of the class filled the screen.

The kids laughed. Some of them had their mouths hanging open. A few were smiling. One or two looked bored.

"This is a snapshot of you," said Mr. Noble. "I could study this picture for days and days and come up with ideas about you as creatures. I could try to explain why some of you were smiling or why some of you look sleepy.

I could talk about the hairstyles you wear. I could draw conclusions about why your knees bend a certain way so you can sit down at desks. I could wonder about the art on the posters hanging on the wall behind you. And some of what I decide about you may be right. Some of what I decide will be wrong. That's because this snapshot isn't complete. It doesn't show me everything I need to know about you: how you live and breathe and walk, or what you do outside of this classroom or what you're thinking."

Nick looked at himself in the photo on the screen. His brow was pushed close together like he was confused.

Mr. Noble said, "Catholics believe that science gives us 'snapshots' of what we know when we know it. But we don't know everything. We learn a lot of things as we go along. There was a time when science thought the sun revolved around the earth. There was a time when science didn't know about atoms or what's on the moon or how the human body works or how trees grow. We keep taking snapshots and add to what we know. That's why Catholics don't panic when science comes up with ideas that don't fit what we believe. We know that new evidence will come along."

Mr. Noble pushed a button. "I'm going to show you what's under that microscope," he said. He pointed to a large microscope next to him. "These are cells from the cheek of my baby daughter."

Nick blinked a couple of times as the screen filled with rough round shapes that looked like little clear chips or blotches of a see-through fluid. Each one had a dot in it and lines that looked like thin veins.

"Science can tell you a lot about

my six-month-old baby girl," Mr. Noble said. "But it can't tell you about her personality or what she's thinking or how she's feeling right now."

Nick stared at the cells on the screen. If he closed his eyes a little, he thought they looked like countries on a map.

Mr. Noble said, "I asked you how big is yellow. Now let me ask, how small is God?"

Nick sat up. He remembered someone else asking him that question once.

Mr. Noble pointed to the screen. "If these were cells from the cheek of the

baby Jesus, would you see God in them?"

Nick gazed at the cells on the screen. *No*, he thought. *We can't see God under a microscope.*

The image turned off. The screen slowly slid up again. The classroom lights brightened.

"I love science," Mr. Noble told the class. "But there are a lot of things science may never be able to prove or explain."

• • •

"How small is God?" Nick asked Brad and Riley at recess. They were outside near the playground. Snow still covered almost everything, but that didn't stop most of the kids from playing on the swings and slide. Nick saw that Sister Lucy's snowman still stood near the corner of the grounds.

"That's a crazy question," Brad said.

"I always thought God was really, really big," said Riley.

"How big?" Nick asked. "As big as the universe?"

"He has to be bigger than that," Brad said.

"Why?" asked Nick.

"Because he's God and he has to be bigger than all the stuff he made," Brad replied.

Riley shook his head. "Can't God be any size he wants to be?" he asked.

Brad kicked at a pile of snow. "Are you guys trying to give me a headache?"

Mr. Norm, the school handyman, stepped out of the school. He walked over to a small shed near one of the walls. Nick was glad he came out.

"Let's ask Mr. Norm," Nick said. He started toward the shed.

"Why?" Brad asked.

"Because he asked me that question once," Nick said.

The three boys surrounded Mr. Norm next to the shed. As usual, he wore overalls and boots and had a toothpick in the corner of his mouth. Today he also had on a plaid overcoat and black gloves.

Mr. Norm said the question back to them. "How small is God?"

"Tell Brad and Riley what you told me," Nick said. He was thinking of a talk they'd had a few months ago.

"Let's see," he said. The toothpick twitched at the corner of his mouth. "God is bigger than anything we know, right? But he became the size of a baby that was made up of atoms and cells and flesh and blood. He grew up like a man but was still God. He looked like one thing while he was something else at the same time. It's like he was God in disguise."

Nick looked at Brad and Riley. Riley's eyebrows were pushed together. He was thinking.

Brad frowned. "God in disguise?" he said.

"He appeared to some people like an angel. He appeared to Moses in the burning bush," Mr. Norm said. "He shows up in a lot of different ways. We don't always recognize him. After Jesus rose from the dead, the women at the tomb thought Jesus was a gardener."

"You're saying Jesus is in disguise in the wafer and wine?" Riley asked.

Brad shuffled his feet. "Why does God have to put on a disguise? Why doesn't he just appear as God?"

Mr. Norm took the toothpick out of his mouth. "How would you react if God just suddenly appeared right in front of you? Do you think you'd just smile and wave? It's the God of the Universe, who is so far beyond our way of thinking and greater than we can imagine and more powerful than our senses of sight, touch, smell, or hearing can handle, and he appears to you as himself? You'd be scared beyond belief."

Brad pressed his lips together. Then he shrugged as an *I guess so.*

"He has to come to us in ways that we can see and understand," Mr. Norm said. "First he came to us as Jesus. And Jesus decided that one of the ways he would be with us after he returned to Heaven would be in a couple of small things: bread and wine."

The boys looked at each other. It sounded so simple when Mr. Norm said it.

Mr. Norm tucked the toothpick back in the corner of his mouth. "What a wonderful mystery," he said.

CHAPTER FIVE

—·—

Twinkles and Twins

On Friday of that week, Sam got permission to do her science project.

Sister Lucy laughed. "I've never seen a project on the impact of science projects on families," she said.

Brad got the okay to do his project on moldy Twinkle Cakes.

Riley wouldn't tell anyone what his project was going to be.

Nick signed up to do the project on rusty nails.

Sister Lucy gave him a knowing look.

"Your father did that one when he was a kid, didn't he?"

Nick blushed. "Yes," he said.

"I've had three other kids ask to do that one," Sister Lucy said. "A lot of parents have done that one. How about a project of your own?"

"Like what?" Nick asked. He hadn't thought of any other projects. He didn't know he'd have to.

Sister Lucy reached into her desk drawer. She pulled out a blue folder and looked inside. She shuffled through some pages. "How about this?" she asked and handed him one of the sheets.

The paper said, *How Do Paper Airplanes Fly?* It had drawings of different kinds of paper airplanes.

"This is a good project for you to try," Sister Lucy said.

Nick knew it would be harder than the rusty nail project. He also knew he had to say yes. So he did.

At lunch, Sam and Kim sat with Nick, Brad, and Riley. Sam thought that Riley kept looking at her. She wanted to ask him why he was doing it. But then she thought she might be wrong.

After they had finished eating, Riley stood up with his cafeteria tray. He turned to get out of his seat and a cup of water tipped off of the tray. The cup spilled onto Nick's lap.

Nick jumped up. The water ran down the front of his shirt and pants. "Hey!" he shouted.

Riley handed him a wad of paper napkins to mop it up. "I'm sorry!" Riley said over and over.

Sam could see that Riley wasn't sorry. She thought he had spilled the water on purpose. *Why would he do that?* she wondered.

"Do you think Riley is acting weird?" Sam asked Kim later.

"I think Riley always acts weird," Kim said. "Do you think he *likes* you?"

"I hope not," Sam said with a groan.

At the end of the school day, Sam went to get her coat from the closet. Riley followed her.

"I feel bad about lunch," he said.

"It was only water," Sam said. She put on her coat and picked up her backpack.

Riley fumbled around with his coat. "Did you know?" he asked.

Sam wasn't sure what he meant. "Know what?"

"Did you know the cup would spill on Nick?" Riley said.

"How would I know that?" Sam asked.

"Because you're his twin," Riley said.

"Like you knew that Brad was going to drop the snow on Nick the other day."

Sam glared at Riley. "Forget about that," she said. She walked away from him.

He followed her, still struggling to get both arms into his coat sleeves. "But you knew, right?" he said.

Sam turned on him. "I know what will happen if you don't leave me alone," she said. She spun around and ran straight into Nick.

"Watch out," he said.

"Tell your friend to go away," she said and marched off.

As she went, she heard Riley ask Nick, "Did you know she was going to run into you?"

• • •

"You're kidding," Nick said to Sam after they got home. "You think Riley's doing his science project about *us*?"

"Yes!" she said. "He spilled that cup

of water on you on purpose. Then he asked if I knew it was going to happen."

"Did you?" Nick asked.

"No," she said.

"I wish you did," Nick said. "I felt soggy all afternoon. And I looked like I wet my pants."

Sam groaned. "I heard him ask if you knew I was going to run into you."

"But I *did*," Nick said. "You were walking straight at me without looking."

"I'll bet he's writing it all down now," Sam said.

"Who cares?" Nick asked. "Why's it bugging you?"

"I don't like being somebody's science project," she said.

• • •

That evening, Mrs. Perry took Sam and Nick to the store to get supplies for their projects. They bought different kinds of paper for Nick's airplanes and construction paper and lettering for the displays.

Mrs. Perry bought Sam a notebook. "You have to keep a diary of all the times and discussions and arguments."

Sam's first entry in the notebook said,

> 7 minutes. Fight about what colors to use for the display paper. Mom wanted white. I wanted yellow. Nick wanted blue.

Sam's second entry in the notebook said,

> 10 minutes. Argued about paper for Nick's airplane project. Nick wanted to buy plastic models to throw off of the roof. Mom said no.

She also remembered to write down about Riley using her and Nick as his science project. She was spending time thinking about that.

She wrote,

> I'm going to find out the truth.

CHAPTER SIX

—·—

Wine and Worries

The next school day Riley cornered Nick in the hallway.

"Is your sister mad at me?" he asked.

"She thinks you're doing your science project about us," Nick said.

"Why would I do that?" Riley asked. His cheeks turned red.

"Because we're twins and you think we have a weird connection," Nick said.

"She warned you about Brad dumping snow on you," Riley said.

"So?"

"She couldn't *see* you," Riley said. His voice rose. It always did when he got excited. "How did she know it was going to happen?"

Nick didn't know what to say.

"Come on," Riley coaxed him. "Other things have happened."

Nick pressed his lips together.

"Don't you see how cool it is?" Riley said. "Twins have something no one else has. It's almost like you're . . . you're superheroes."

Superheroes? Nick thought.

"I'll bet things happen to you two all the time," Riley said.

Nick looked around to make sure no one was listening. "Do you remember when I saw that mountain lion?" he said.

"Yeah."

Nick went on, "And when you broke through the ice and I went in to get you?"

"Uh huh."

"Both times Sam said she knew something bad was happening," Nick said.

"*Really*?" Riley squealed.

"Keep your voice down," Nick said. "You can't tell her I told you."

Riley's eyes were big. His mouth had turned into a big *O*. He said, "I knew it! You guys are amazing!"

It is incredible, Nick thought. "But you can't do your science project about us," Nick said as firmly as he could.

"Let's go, boys!" Father Cliff said. He hurried them toward the door.

The two boys went into the class.

Sister Lucy had a box on her desk. She took out a long loaf of bread. She handed it to Father Cliff.

"Bread," Father Cliff said. He handed it to Elena at the first desk. "Take a look and pass it around," he told her.

Next came a box of salt. Then a book about birds. Then a packet of seeds. Then some oranges and grapes and apples.

"Jesus used everyday events and

things to teach about the mysteries of
the Faith," Father Cliff said. "He told
stories about fathers, mothers, sons,
daughters, widows, farmers, travelers,
tradesmen, rebels, kings, and criminals.
He said things like, 'Look at the birds of
the air, the flowers of the field.' He talked
about seeds of the ground and vineyards
and fruit and rocks and sand. He used
dirt and spit to allow a blind man to see.
He knew people would understand if he
used the things they knew about."

He went to the board and wrote down the words "Bread" and "Wine."

"You'll find stories about bread and wine throughout the Bible," Father Cliff said. "It was used for honor and blessings. And do you remember what 'manna' is?"

Riley raised his hand. "It was the bread God sent to Israel so they wouldn't starve," he said.

"Very good," Father Cliff said. "Can any of you remember stories about Jesus and wine?"

Kim raised her hand. "Jesus went to a wedding and turned water into wine," she said.

Father Cliff smiled at her. "That's right. The Gospel of John, chapter 2. In Jesus's time, weddings were a big event that lasted for hours. There was a huge feast with a lot of food and wine. It's the kind of event where everything needs to be just right. But something went wrong."

More raised hands. A boy named Derek said, "They ran out of wine."

"Running out of wine at a wedding was so embarrassing!" Father Cliff said. "It was a big problem. But Mary, the mother of Jesus, found out. What did she do?"

"She told Jesus to fix the problem," Sam said.

"You mean, she told him to run to the store to buy some more?" Father Cliff asked.

Some of the kids laughed.

Sam said, "Jesus had the servants bring out six huge jars."

"These were jars as big as you," said Father Cliff. "He told them to fill the jars with water. They held gallons and gallons. After they were filled up, Jesus said to take a cup to the man in charge of the wedding. So they did. The man tasted it and said it was great-tasting wine."

Father Cliff clapped his hands together. "Jesus showed that he had the power to change one thing into something else. Keep that in mind until next time."

The lesson was over. Father Cliff put all the items back into the box. "Next week we're taking a little field trip," Father Cliff said. "We're going to the Hope Springs Museum."

A wave of excitement moved around the class.

Nick wondered what the museum had to do with their First Communion.

•••

Nick was worried about Riley. He had a bad feeling that he shouldn't have said anything about the twin thing. *Sam will be furious*, he thought. *"We'll be like Big Foot to him," she'll say.*

He watched Riley at lunch. He braced himself for when Riley would do or say something to Sam. But he didn't.

Only one strange thing happened in the afternoon. Riley came up to Nick and said, "Pick a number between one and ten."

"Seven," Nick said.

"Thanks," Riley said and walked away.

Later on at home, Mr. Perry reminded Nick more than once to start his science project.

Nick went to his room and took out the paper for his airplanes. The sheets were of different weights and thicknesses.

He considered how he needed to fold each one. It seemed like a lot of work.

His eye caught the spine of a book on the shelf about real airplanes. He pulled it down and flipped through the pages to look at the pictures. He liked the Spitfires from World War II and the F-16 that some called the "Fighting Falcon" and the Sopwith Camel from World War I.

He lost track of time until Sam came into the room.

"Hi," she said.

He tossed the book onto his desk. "I'm doing it," he said.

"Doing what?" she asked.

"My science project. I was looking at that book for ideas," Nick said.

She held up her diary. "How long have you been working on it?"

"A while," he said. "I can't remember."

She opened the diary and held her pencil over the page. "Fifteen minutes? An hour?" she asked.

"A half hour," he said.

"How many times did Dad have to ask you to do it?" she asked.

"Only once," Nick said. "*Twice*," he corrected himself, then, "Three times."

Sam wrote it down.

Nick fell onto his bed. "Putting the nails in jars would have been a lot easier."

Sam said, "Maybe that's why Sister Lucy didn't want you to do it."

"It's not like *your* project is hard," he

complained. "All you have to do is watch and write things down. Just like Riley. He's watching us. You're watching me. That's easy."

"It's not easy to sneak around like he does," Sam said.

"He wasn't sneaking around today," Nick said. "Maybe we're not his science project after all."

"Except, he asked me to pick a number between one and ten," Sam said.

Uh oh, Nick thought. "Maybe it was just a game. What number did you say?"

"Seven," Sam said.

Nick pondered whether or not to tell Sam that he'd picked the same number. He decided not to. Instead, he asked, "Why's it so bad if he did his science project about us?"

"I don't want to become a freak show at the school," she said.

"We won't be a freak show," Nick countered. "People might think we're cool."

"People will tease us," she said. "They'll do things to test us to see if you know what's happening to me or I know what's happening to you or what we're thinking—"

She suddenly stopped. Her eyes narrowed as if an idea came to her. "Pick a number from one to ten," she said.

Nick swallowed hard.

"*That's* why he asked me to do it," she said. "Did he ask you the same thing?"

Nick turned to the sheets of paper on his desk. He moved one a little to the left and then to the right again for no reason at all. "Yeah," he admitted.

"Another test!" Sam growled.

"Don't make such a big deal out of it," Nick said.

Sam was fuming. "What number did you pick?" she asked.

"Seven," Nick said.

"The same as me! Oh *great*!" Sam said.

"That's going to make him try even more."

"It's not such a bad thing," Nick said.

"Yes, it is!" She stormed out of the room.

"Don't forget to write it in your diary!" Nick shouted after her.

• • •

Sam's project diary entry before she went to bed:

5 minutes. Dad nagged Nick.

30 minutes. Nick worked on paper planes. Not really. He looked at a book about real planes.

5 minutes. Fought about Riley's project.

20 minutes. Angry about Riley's project.

Chapter Seven

——•——

Pencils and Potato Chips

Sam tried to avoid Riley at school. She sat at the desk next to his. She hoped he wouldn't talk to her if she didn't make eye contact.

"Sam," Riley whispered to her later in the morning.

"Leave me alone," she said.

"My pencil fell under your feet," he said. "May I have it back?"

Sam looked down at her feet. A pencil was there. She picked it up. "This isn't a test, is it?" she asked him.

"It was an accident," he said. "Why are you being so mean?"

She handed him the pencil and turned back to her book. *It's a trick,* she thought. *Somehow that pencil is part of his science project. But that's nutty. What does the pencil have to do with me or Nick?*

Then she took out her science project diary. She wrote:

Riley is driving me crazy.

• • •

Father Cliff stood in front of the class. It was time for another lesson about their First Communion.

He held up a small bag of potato chips from the cafeteria. "What would you think if I said that the entire class had to share this small bag of potato chips? Do you think there'd be any left after this first row ate some? Do you think there'd be any left over after the bag reached the last person in the last seat?"

The kids said no.

Father Cliff handed the bag to Sister Lucy. She said, "I'll give this to the student who asks the best question or answers the hardest one."

"We learned about Jesus turning water into wine," Father Cliff said. "Now let's go to chapter 6 in the Gospel of Saint John. Here we find that Jesus arrived on the shore of the Sea of Galilee. Do you remember any stories about the Sea of Galilee?"

Kim raised her hand. "Jesus walked on water there," she said.

Father Cliff nodded to her.

"Peter tried to walk on water there, too," said Sam.

"And Jesus calmed the storm," said a boy named Devon.

"Good answers," Father Cliff said. "And it was near here that Jesus began his earthly ministry. Peter, Andrew, James, and John were fishermen there. Matthew was a tax collector in that same area. Jesus healed a lot of people there, too."

Father Cliff began to walk up and down the aisles of desks. "It wasn't a big surprise that people followed him when he showed up there. He went up a mountain with his disciples and a lot of people tagged along. Do you know how many people were there?"

Lance raised his hand and said, "Five thousand!"

"Five thousand *men*," Father Cliff told them. "More if you add the women and children. Think about how many people that is. It's like a town full of people."

Father Cliff looked up at the clock. "It's almost lunchtime. Are you hungry?"

A few of the kids said yes.

"Well," said Father Cliff, "Scripture tells us that suppertime came, and

Jesus knew the people would be hungry. He turned to one of his disciples, Philip, and said, 'How are we going to get bread to feed these people?'

"You can imagine the reaction. 'We don't have enough money to buy food for all these people!' Philip said. Jesus already knew that. He knew what he had planned. And then Andrew, the brother of Peter, said, 'Here's a boy that has five barley loaves and two fish.' It was a joke. You can't feed thousands of people with five loaves of cheap bread and two fish. It's like expecting that small bag of potato chips to feed this class. So what did Jesus do?"

"He told everyone to sit down," a boy named Brandon said.

Father Cliff waved his hands like he was telling people to sit down. "That's right. Jesus had everyone sit down. He took the five loaves and two fish and prayed over them. He blessed the food.

Then he told his disciples to hand out the food. And they did."

Father Cliff went to Sister Lucy's desk and picked up the small bag of potato chips. "What would you think if I told you to pass around this bag and to eat as much as you wanted? You'd think I was crazy. But what would you do if the bag went from person to person and it didn't wasn't empty? What if we got to the last person and poured out what was left and it filled a dozen boxes with potato chips?"

Father Cliff paused. He made his way down the aisles again. "That's what happened. Eventually, *everyone* was fed. Everyone. They had *twelve baskets* of leftovers."

"Was that one basket for each disciple?" Riley asked.

Father Cliff laughed. "Good question!"

Sister Lucy gave Riley the bag of potato chips. "You win," she said.

Father Cliff walked to the front of the class again. "It was no magic trick. He didn't have fish and bread stuck up his sleeves. The food wasn't hidden under some blankets or secretly buried nearby. He took a couple of ordinary things and did something that only God could do."

He let the kids think about it for a minute.

"It's one thing for Jesus to turn water into wine," he said. "It's another to take a few loaves and a couple of fish and multiply them into *thousands.* It's impossible! But Jesus did it. Jesus did things like that all the time. He stopped a storm at sea. He walked on water. He cured people who suffered from incurable sicknesses. He constantly controlled nature, doing supernatural things to glorify his Father in Heaven. He looked normal, but he was God. He looked like one thing, but he was so much more than what he appeared to be. That's what I want you to think about until next time."

• • •

At recess, Sam went with Kim to one of the picnic tables near the playground. They pushed the last of the snow from the seats and sat down.

Kim looked down at the crystals stuck on her mittens. "They say that every snowflake is different."

"How do they know that?" Sam said.

Kim brushed her mittens together to knock the snow away. "Maybe they pay people to double-check."

Sam laughed. "Every time it snows people rush out to capture the flakes and look at them under microscopes."

The two girls giggled.

Sam watched the kids running around on the playground. "I guess it's like people," she said. "We're all alike, but we're all different."

Sam thought about Jesus and the miracle of the loaves and fishes. *Jesus looked like a normal human being, but he was completely different*, she thought.

"Watch out!" Sam heard Brad shout.

Sam shifted just a little to her left. A ball whooshed past her head and hit the table top. It bounced and flew into a group of kids by the school door. Kim screeched.

Riley rushed up to them. "I'm sorry," he said, panting. "It was a wild kick."

He got the ball from the kids and ran back to play.

"Sorry!" he said as he darted past them.

"That was close," Kim said. "Now I have to make my heart beat again."

Sam looked around. "Where's Nick?" she asked.

Kim pointed to the other end of the playground. "He's over there," she said.

Sam looked up. Nick was walking around the snowman Sister Lucy had made. He was patting new snow into the side of it.

"Why?" Kim asked her.

"Just wondering," Sam said. But she wasn't just wondering. "I thought the ball was another test from Riley."

Kim looked puzzled. "A test?"

"To see if twins can sense danger and warn each other," Sam said.

"Can they—I mean, *you*. Can you?" Kim asked.

Sam nodded. "I think Riley has made

it his science project."

Kim looked even more puzzled. "But Brad warned you, not Nick."

"Yeah, but Riley kicked the ball," Sam said.

"What if Brad or Nick didn't say anything?" Kim said. She sounded annoyed. "I don't think Sister Lucy wants anyone to get hurt for a science project."

Sam looked at her friend. "If Riley asks Nick about the ball coming at me, then I'll know it was a test. If it is, I'm going to talk to Sister Lucy."

• • •

"I heard you had a close call today," Nick said to Sam while they waited for their mom in the afternoon carpool.

Lizzy was standing nearby. "What close call?" she asked.

Sam explained to her about the ball that nearly hit her.

"You think Riley did it on purpose?"

Lizzy asked.

"For his science project," Sam said. She explained her suspicions.

Lizzy listened. She said, "That's a clever idea."

"I think so, too," Nick said.

Sam turned to her. "You think it's a good idea?"

"I said it was clever," Lizzy said. "I don't think it's a good idea unless you agree to help."

"You're taking Riley's side?" Sam said unhappily.

"I'm not taking sides," Lizzy said. "I just said it was a good idea for a science project. But he shouldn't do it if you don't want to."

Sam faced Nick. "How did you hear about the close call?"

"Riley and Brad were fighting about it," Nick said. He shoved his hands into his coat pocket and shuffled from one leg to the other. "It's cold," he said.

"Why were they fighting?" Sam asked.

Nick gave a small shrug. "I think Riley was mad because Brad warned you the ball was coming."

Sam grunted. "He wanted me to get hit?"

"No. He wanted *me* to warn you," Nick said.

Sam could feel the anger rise within her. "Did Riley ask if you knew I was about to get hit?"

Nick looked bothered. "Brad asked. But I think Riley put him up to it."

Sam stomped her feet on the pavement. "That's it. I'm going to talk to Sister Lucy."

Nick growled. "I wish you'd calm down. Riley thinks twins are cool."

"I get it," Sam said. "You think everyone will say we're cool if Riley does this project."

"Yeah," Nick said.

"Talk to Mom and Dad about it," Lizzy suggested.

Their mom pulled the family van into

the parking lot. Sam saw Andrew run from the playground. He jumped into the front passenger seat.

Nick opened the back door to the van. He moved aside for Lizzy to get in. Sam was about to follow, but Nick put his hand on her arm. "I didn't tell them," he said.

"Tell them what?" Sam asked.

"Get in," Mrs. Perry said. "It's cold!"

The twins climbed onto the seat. They dropped their backpacks at their feet. Nick closed the door. They buckled in.

"I knew about the ball," Nick said softly. "I was trying to fix Sister Lucy's snowman when I got that funny feeling. You know. I looked up and saw what was about to happen. I started to yell at you, but Brad did it first. So I pretended I didn't know."

"If Riley finds out, he'll never leave us alone." Sam slumped into her seat as if her entire body had become a pout.

"We're like a Big Foot project to him."

"It's not that bad," Nick said.

"It's a good thing he doesn't know what happened with the mountain lion or the ice," Sam said.

Sam thought she heard a loud *gulp* come from Nick.

"Is something wrong?" Mrs. Perry asked from the front.

Sam grunted.

"Can we talk about it at home?" Nick asked.

—·—

Chapter Eight

Freaks and Family Talk

The discussion turned into a family meeting after dinner. Sam and Nick explained Riley's science project to their parents, Andrew, and Lizzy.

"You don't know for sure he's doing the project about you," Mr. Perry said.

"It sure sounds like he is," said Mrs. Perry. "But we can ask Sister Lucy."

"I think it's okay," Nick said.

"I don't like it," Sam said. "We're like freaks."

"Or really cool superheroes," Nick said.

"You both may be right," Mr. Perry said. "Some of the kids will think it's cool. Some will think it's weird."

"It's an invasion of privacy," Sam said.

"That's fair," Mrs. Perry said. "We'll put a stop to it if you want. Do you want me to talk to Sister Lucy?"

Sam felt like she was put on the spot. "Yes, please. No, wait. Maybe. I don't know."

Lizzy was sitting with her sketch pad, as usual. Sam thought she was drawing a picture of the family. Lizzy looked up. She asked, "Do twins have a special bond?"

Mr. and Mrs. Perry looked at each other.

Mrs. Perry said, "The truth is, we saw hints of it when you were babies. There were times when you seemed to be talking to each other without speaking. When one of you got hurt in one part of the house, the other cried in another part of the house."

"We talked to doctors and specialists," Mr. Perry said. "Many of them believed twins do have an unusual connection."

"No one can explain why," Mrs. Perry added. "It's a mystery."

Lizzy cleared her throat gently. She said to Nick and Sam, "I was thinking. Your class is learning about the Body and Blood of Jesus now, right?"

"Yeah," said Nick.

"Maybe your special 'twin' sense will help some of the other kids," Lizzy said.

"How?" asked Mr. Perry.

"Because it's a mystery," Lizzy replied. "Just like the Body and Blood are mysteries. We can't really understand them. We have to take them by faith."

Mrs. Perry shook her head. "I don't think that what happens with Sam and Nick is anything like the Body and Blood of Jesus."

Sam agreed. "We're weird. The Body

and Blood are supposed to be a miracle."

All eyes went back to Lizzy for a response. She looked like she was having a hard time finding the right words to say.

Andrew suddenly spoke up. "I know what Lizzy means," he said. "When we were little, you told us stories about Peter Pan flying and genies coming out of lamps and magic castles and mermaids and all kinds of amazing places. Why did you tell us those stories?"

"Because we wanted you to use your imaginations," Mr. Perry said.

"Why?" Andrew asked again.

"Because learning to use our imaginations helps us to accept what we can't understand," Mr. Perry replied. "Our imaginations help make the impossible seem possible."

Lizzy raised her hand.

"You're not in class," Mrs. Perry said with a smile.

Lizzy said slowly, "I believe in Jesus and angels and Heaven and miracles and the sacraments because I believed a magic wardrobe could take kids to Narnia."

"But those stories aren't real," Mrs. Perry said.

"I know," said Lizzy. She struggled to find her words again.

Andrew spoke up again, "Believing those stories *could* happen helped us believe the stories of Jesus *did* happen. I think that's what Lizzy is trying to say."

Lizzy nodded. She gave Andrew a little smile of thanks. "If the kids see a science project and think it's possible for twins to have a mysterious bond, then it might be easier for them to believe that Jesus is really in the bread and wine."

Mr. Perry sat back on the sofa. "That's an interesting thought."

Mrs. Perry turned to him and said playfully, "Where did these kids come from?"

He smiled then held his hands as if to say he didn't know.

"What are we supposed to do?" asked Nick.

"It's up to you, Sam," Mrs. Perry said to her daughter.

"But you have to decide quickly," said Mr. Perry. "It's unfair for Riley to have to start a new project."

"I will," Sam said. But she was already wondering if Riley's project really would help some of the kids have faith.

• • •

Later that evening Sam wrote in her project diary:

20 minutes. Family talk about Riley's project.

1 hour. Bedtime. Sat in my room and worried about it.

Chapter Nine

—·—

Perrys and Pyrite

Morning came, and spring seemed to tag along with it. The air had a hint of a new warmth. The sun seemed brighter somehow. Sam almost expected flowers to burst up from the ground.

Sam decided to talk to Kim about Riley's project.

During the morning assembly, Father Cliff announced that he would be *walking* Sister Lucy's and Sister Monica's third-grade classes to the Hope Springs Museum downtown. Gasps and whispers went through the assembly hall.

Sister Lucy guided her students back to class to put on their coats. She reminded them how they were to walk to the museum. "You each have a walking buddy," she said.

Kim Lee was Sam's walking buddy in front. Nick was her walking buddy behind her. Behind Nick was Brad. Riley was behind Brad.

"Wait for me at the crosswalks and intersections," Sister Lucy said.

It was a ten-minute walk from the school. They walked past small shops and large yards surrounded by short fences with big houses behind them. Some people called this area the "Old Neighborhood" because most of the homes were built when the town began to grow.

Sam gazed over at one house she knew well. She turned to Nick. He was looking, too. They slowed down to look.

The house sat behind a tall iron fence. A gate opened to a long driveway that stretched back through a line of oak trees to a funny-looking house made of brick. It was funny-looking because it was like a collection of uneven boxes. One section had two stories, then rose up to three stories in the next section, and down to one story in another section. A long porch along the front wrapped around the sides. It was like a belt that held the various parts together.

On one side of the house was a round tower with an open balcony on the top floor. On the other side was an octagonal wing with large bay windows.

The whole thing had a lot of roofs that jutted up like the letter *A* over each section and smaller ones over the windows. Chimneys stuck up here and there. Sam thought it was like looking at a mountain range.

The wood railings along the porch and around the windows had lines and curves that reminded Sam of flowers and butterfly wings.

The twins were looking at the house because their father grew up there. Uncle Clark, their father's older brother, still lived there. It was called "The Old Perry House." Uncle Clark called it "The Old Monster."

The Perry family often stayed there when they visited Hope Springs from Denver. They didn't visit very often now. Uncle Clark was always up on the mountain. He was building a new resort for the town.

Sam thought about the hallways that angled this way and that, and the different rooms tucked away in surprising places. She missed the Old Perry House. She wished she lived there.

"Let's keep moving!" Sister Lucy called out.

Sam realized she and Nick were holding up the line. They started walking again.

The kids marched into the downtown area of Hope Springs. Sam walked past the Royal Hotel and saw the signs for the hot springs in the back. The old train station sat down a side road, but it was now filled with shops. She saw the Hayes building. It used to be a five-story department store but now had expensive condos. The Coliseum Cinema was showing the movie *Ben Hur*. The Perry family had watched it at home on Easter Sunday afternoon.

They stopped at an intersection. Bob the Policeman was directing traffic. He stopped all the cars and allowed them to cross. They came to a big lawn with a fountain. Past that was the Hope Springs City Hall. It was a huge brick building with tall white pillars along the front and a dome on the top. The Hope Springs

Museum was housed in a side wing.

Sister Lucy led them to a room where they could hang up their coats. Then they went into a room that stretched the length of the whole building. There they met Sally the Guide. Sally looked like a teenager. She had long blonde hair and a bright smile. She wore a bright red shirt that said, "Hope Springs Alive."

"Sally will take you around to the displays," Sister Lucy said.

"I'm so glad you're here!" Sally said as she waved for them to follow her.

Sally walked them to exhibits of artifacts from Native American tribes and Spanish and Mexican missionaries. Sam saw in one of the glass cases that some of the artifacts came from Uncle Clark's resort. Uncle Clark's workers had found the site of a mission from a long time ago and dug up cups and plates and crosses and even part of an old prayer book.

Sally showed them a real supply wagon from the mid-1800s. It belonged to the U.S. Calvary when the soldiers had been posted near Hope Springs. There was a history of trains with a running model train set. An exhibit about the hot springs told how the waters brought sick people looking for healing.

The kids reached a vast wall of black-and-white pictures that showed the history of Hope Springs. Sam saw wooden sidewalks that ran along small shacks of stores. Horse-drawn carriages and wagons were spread out on the main road. The hot springs had people in funny bathing suits sitting in folding chairs around the edge, with a half-built Royal Hotel in the background. Men in top hats and women in big dresses and umbrellas stood in front of the City Hall. There were photos of famous people from the past like actors Douglas Fairbanks,

Lon Chaney, comedian Will Rogers, a movie cowboy named Tom Mix, and the real cowboy Wyatt Earp that stood on the platform at the train station.

Sam noticed that one of the pictures was of a fancy dinner for Theodore Roosevelt at the Perry House in 1912. She thought she recognized her ancestor Arthur Perry. He had a large mustache and wore a tuxedo. He was standing next to Theodore Roosevelt.

Sally the Guide led them back to a large room dedicated to the mining in the mountains around Hope Springs. There were photos of miners wearing candles in their hats and prospectors kneeling along riverbanks. Sally told them how the prospectors spent long days searching the mountains for gold and silver. They would dig holes in the dirt and filter the rocks and pebbles into large buckets. Then they carried the buckets to a stream and put small

amounts in pans. They slowly washed the pans in the water, moving the water back and forth and spinning it around to separate the dirt from the heavier gold that might settle on the bottom.

"How would you like to pan for gold?" Sally asked them.

The kids raised their hands and jumped up and down.

"Come on," Sally said and took them to another room. Large pieces of mining equipment hung on the walls. In the corner was an actual caged elevator that took men down into the mines. A long trough ran the length of a wall. Sam could hear trickling water.

"It's not a real river, but it's close," said Sally. The kids were given small flat bowls and told to step onto a rail next to the trough. Water gently ran from one end to the other. The bottom of the trough was thick with dirt and rocks.

"You can pan this little river," Sally the Guide said. "We change the bed of the trough every few days with earth from the mountains. There's every chance you'll find some real gold."

Sally showed them how to scoop the pans along the bottom of the sink, then carefully swish the rock and dirt around the pan to find gold. "Take your time. Most people hope to find big rocks of gold. Experienced prospectors know to look for smaller nuggets and flakes. They knew that a little could lead to a lot."

Sam pushed up her sleeves and

looked at the water. She wondered if she'd find real gold in the dirt beneath.

"By the way," Sally said with an excited voice, "You can keep any gold you find!"

The kids were more willing to try. Sam scooped up small rocks and pebbles. She lifted the pan. The water swished around and around.

Father Cliff came up behind her. "Tilt the pan so the water and the rocks spill back into the water. Sift it a little at a time. Keep your eyes on it."

Sam did what he said. Brown dirt and rocks slipped out. Soon she had fine grains and smaller lumps in the bottom of the pan. She looked close but couldn't see any gold.

"I found some!" Nick cried out.

Sam turned to him, "Really?"

Nick held up a rock. It had speckles of yellow in it.

Sally the Guide came around to see.

"I'm sorry. That isn't gold."

"It *looks* like gold," Nick said.

"You found some 'fool's gold,'" Sally explained. She held up the rock for all to see. "Do you know why it's called 'fool's gold'?"

"Because it looks like gold but really isn't," said Riley.

"Very good," Sally said. "This is called 'pyrite.' It's a mineral that has a kind of brassy yellow color. Prospectors thought it was gold, too. Then they learned to smell it. If it smelled like sulphur, then it was fool's gold. Or they might tap it with a hammer. If it broke in pieces, it was fool's good. If it flattened or expanded, then it was probably gold."

"Is it worth anything?" Nick asked.

"Not much," Sally said. "I'm sorry."

In the end, Father Cliff thanked Sally the Guide for all her help. Then he said to the kids, "You saw a lot today. Hope

Springs has a wonderful history. But I want you to think about the fool's gold. It's something that looks like one thing but wasn't. Next time we meet, I'm going to show you something that's the other way around."

Sam wondered what he meant.

• • •

On the walk back to St. Clare's, Sam moved close to Kim. She told her about the decision she had to make.

Kim bowed her head. She sometimes did that when she was thinking. It looked like she was praying. Maybe she was.

"Do you think it will help some of the kids believe in the Eucharist?" Sam asked.

Kim wore a knitted cap with two strings on each side. The strings dangled down like floppy ears. She lifted her head again. "I don't know," she finally said.

They walked on quietly for a moment.

Sam asked, "What would *you* do?"

"I'd talk to Sister Lucy," Kim said. "She'll know the right thing to do."

Sam asked Sister Lucy if they could talk after school.

"Of course," Sister Lucy said.

Sam told Nick. They both waited until the rest of the class left for the day. Brad and Riley lingered at the door until Nick waved at them to go away.

Sister Lucy sat at her desk. "What's going on?" she asked.

Sam began by asking if Riley was doing his science project about twins.

"It's true," Sister Lucy said to Sam and Nick. "He asked to do his project about twins. But I told him he may not mention your names or present anything that's personal."

"But we're the only twins in our class," Sam said. "Everyone will know it's us."

"Are you worried about that?" Sister Lucy asked.

Sam hesitated.

"I'm not," Nick said.

Sam shot him an unhappy look. "Riley keeps doing little tests. It's bugging me."

"I'm sorry about that. He was supposed to talk to you about it," Sister Lucy said. "I told him to figure out how to conduct *real* tests with you."

"I probably scared him off," Sam admitted.

Sister Lucy looked at Sam. "We can change his project. Is that what you want?"

Sam twisted the bottom of her sweater. She did that when she was nervous. She told Sister Lucy about the talk her family had the night before.

Sister Lucy listened and then said, "It's hard to know if a science project about the mystery of twins will help kids with the Eucharist. But it's a sweet idea. I know grown-ups who say they became

Christians because they read stories that inspired their imaginations. Some scientists became Christians because of the mysteries of nature."

Sam didn't know what to do.

"Aren't you curious to see a science project on why twins seem to have a special sense?" Sister Lucy asked.

"I am," said Nick.

Sam shrugged. "I'm not sure it's a special sense at all," she said. "Maybe it's just coincidence."

Sister Lucy folded her hands in front of her. "How about this: let's test the idea. That's what Riley's project is supposed to do. Real tests. No more sneaking around. We'll do them together in private. I'll talk to your parents to make sure it's all right."

"What kind of tests?" Sam asked.

Sister Lucy said, "We could put you in one room and Nick in another and try some physical tests."

"Physical?" Nick asked. He looked concerned.

"Nothing hard," Sister Lucy said. "Maybe we'll place your hand in some cold water to see if Sam has the same feeling in the other room."

"We've never had that happen," Nick said.

"Yes we did," Sam corrected him. "Remember when we were little? You reached up and touched that hot pan. I was in the other room and felt burning in my fingers."

Nick thought about it. "Mom was making brownies. I wanted one fresh out of the oven."

Sam asked Sister Lucy, "How can I feel something that he feels somewhere else?"

"We live in a world of mysteries." Sister Lucy said. Then she pushed her chair back and stood up. "Would you like to see a mystery?"

"Yes," the twins said.

"Put on your coats and follow me," she said.

The twins obeyed. They followed Sister Lucy down the hall to a door that led outside. It took them to a side of the school that they hardly saw. It had a stretch of lawn that was too thin to use for anything practical. She led them across the patches of snow to the wooden fence.

She bent down and pointed. "See?"

Sam and Nick bent down, too.

A red rose stuck up through the snow.

"It's beautiful," Sam said.

"Did you put that there?" Nick asked.

"No. The school doesn't plant flowers along this fence. It's too much trouble for Mr. Norm when he cuts the grass."

Sam knelt closer and looked at one side of the rose, then the other. She had heard of a flower that bloomed in the snow. "Is this a winter rose?"

Sister Lucy shook her head. "It's a normal rose."

"But I thought they died in the snow," said Nick.

"Not this one." Sister Lucy stepped back from the flower.

"Why not?" Sam asked.

"That's the mystery," Sister said with a smile. "We don't know why a rose like this can grow in the winter, but it does."

• • •

That night Sam wrote in her project diary:

We live in a world of mysteries.

Then she wrote:

I hour. Nick and I worked on Nick's project. Dad taught Nick how to make a paper airplane. Nick wanted to make an F-16. Dad told him to keep it simple. Nick argued. Dad got annoyed and gave up. Nick pouted.

10 minutes. I wondered what kinds of tests Riley will do on us.

CHAPTER TEN

—— • ——

Bread and Breakfast

The next morning Sister Lucy's third-grade class walked into a surprise.

In the front of the room was a table set for a fancy meal. There were plates with slices of bread and jars of jam, a teapot, a block of cheese, a basket of eggs, a small sausage and strip of bacon, silverware, a butter tray, napkins, and a small rack with half-slices of toast in it.

"Are we having breakfast?" Brad asked as he walked past the table.

Sister Lucy smiled. She said, "Sit down

and you'll find out."

Nick was curious about the strange display.

A moment after everyone was seated, Father Cliff walked in. He thanked Sister Lucy for setting up the table. Then he turned to the class and asked, "What do you think of our setup?"

Elena raised her hand. "Why is it here?" she asked.

"Come and see," he said to her.

Elena stood up and went to the table.

"Pick up that slice of bread," Father Cliff told her.

She looked unsure.

"Go on," Sister Lucy said.

Elena began to pick up a slice of bread. An odd look crossed her face. She reached down with her other hand and had to use both to pick up the bread. "It's really heavy," she said.

"But it's only a slice of bread, isn't it?" Father Cliff asked.

Elena shook her head. "It's not bread."

Father Cliff took the slice of bread from her. He held it up for the class to see. "It looks like a slice of bread, but it's made of silver."

He dropped it onto the table. It made a loud thump.

"The eggs in that bowl are made of marble. So are the butter and the butter tray," he told them.

He picked up a small strip of bacon. It was brown with white stripes. "This looks good enough to eat. But you can't. It's made of pure gold."

Father Cliff put the bacon back on the plate. He pretended to lick his fingers. The class laughed.

"Everything you see on this table is not what it appears to be," he said. "All of this was made by a friend of mine. He's an artist in Denver. He puts together displays for the art museum. You see? From the outside, it looks like

one thing, but the substance of it is something else."

Father Cliff moved away from the table to Sister Lucy's desk. "We talked about how Jesus turned one liquid into another kind of liquid: water into wine. Then we talked about how Jesus took five loaves and two fish and turned them into hundreds of loaves and fishes."

He leaned against Sister Lucy's desk. "After that, people followed Jesus because he fed them. But he wanted them to think beyond their stomachs.

There was a deeper truth he wanted them to understand. So, what does he tell them? He says to stop working so hard for the kind of food that doesn't last. He says to work for the food that will give them eternal life. Can you think of any food that can give you eternal life?"

Brad raised his hand. He said, "Twinkle Cakes last forever."

Everyone laughed.

Father Cliff grinned. "*Besides* Twinkle Cakes."

The kids were quiet. Nick couldn't think of anything.

"*Nothing* in this world lasts forever," Father Cliff said. "The fish and bread Jesus gave to all those people would eventually spoil. Jesus tells them that God wants them all to have bread from *Heaven*, the true bread that can give them life. And the people say, 'Give us this bread!' Maybe they were thinking,

'What a deal! The guy who fed us all that bread and fish is now offering free meals every day!'"

Nick thought, *That really would be a good deal.*

"Here's where it gets really crazy," Father Cliff said. "Jesus tells them that *he* is the Bread of Life. He says, 'Come to me and you won't hunger. Believe in me and you won't thirst.' The crowd says *'What?'* And he explains how he came from Heaven to do God's will and will raise those who believe in him to eternal life. How do you think they reacted?"

"They got mad," Sam said.

"They were *furious!*" Father Cliff clarified. "Here's Jesus, a man many of them had known for years. He was the son of Joseph and Mary. Now he was claiming to be God's Chosen One who came down from Heaven? He's promising them eternal life? Only *God* could give eternal life. Was Jesus out of his mind?"

Nick shuffled in his seat. It made him feel nervous that people thought Jesus was crazy.

Father Cliff was on his feet again. He moved around the room. "So now the discussion gets really hot. They argue with Jesus about who he is and what he claims he can do. Does Jesus back off? No. He goes even further. He says, 'I am the living bread which came down from Heaven. If anyone eats this bread, he will live forever.'" Father Cliff stopped again. "Do you remember what *kind* of bread he then said he'd give to the world? Was it whole wheat? Maybe a healthy grain? Enriched white bread?"

Some of the kids chuckled. Nick tried to remember the story but drew a blank.

"Jesus says, 'The bread I give for the life of the world is my *flesh.*'" Father Cliff was on the move again. "Just think about that. Eat his flesh! How insane is that? That's what they're thinking. You're probably thinking the same thing now. We're not supposed to eat people's flesh. Why would he say something like that?"

Again, the kids were quiet. No one tried to answer.

Father Cliff went to the window. His hands were clasped behind his back. The day was bright outside. "This is the moment when Jesus should explain himself. This is where Jesus should say, 'I don't mean it. It's symbolic. It's like when I talk about being a vine or a door or a lamb. I don't really mean it.' But Jesus doesn't say that. He makes the situation even worse and says very clearly: 'Unless you eat the flesh of the Son of Man and drink his blood you have no life in you. He who eats my flesh and drinks my blood has eternal life, and I will raise him up at the last day. For my flesh is food indeed, and my blood is drink indeed.'"

Father Cliff paused. "Those are the words of Jesus," he said. "The Church didn't make them up. It's not one of those beliefs somebody with a long Latin name decided would be a fun way to confuse us. Jesus said it. And that was the last straw for the crowd. They'd had enough. They took off."

Nick imagined Jesus standing there while all of those people walked away. It made him feel a little sad.

"Jesus didn't shout for them to come back," Father Cliff reminded them. "He didn't say it was all a misunderstanding. He told them the truth and they walked off. And there are a lot of people like that today. They can't understand it. They can't accept it by faith. So they walk away." Father Cliff drifted to the front of the class again. "Did *everyone* leave?"

Another hand went up. "The disciples stayed," said a girl named Angela.

Father Cliff gave her a thumbs-up for her answer. "The disciples were still there. So Jesus turned and asked them, 'Will you also go away?' And what did Peter say? Did he say, 'Yes, Lord, we completely understand that somehow a wafer and wine can become your Precious Body and Blood and so we'll stay'? No. Peter said, 'Lord, to whom shall we go? You have the words of eternal life. We believe that you are the Holy One of God.'"

Nick wondered if he would have said the same thing if he had been there. *Maybe I would have walked away*, he thought.

"I have a confession," Father Cliff said. "I don't understand how the wafer and wine become the Body and Blood of Jesus. I can't explain the reasons Jesus decided to share himself with us like that. All I know is that Jesus loves me. He shed his blood and broke his body for me. He feeds me and offers eternal life to me in the Eucharist. I don't understand it, but I accept it by faith."

Father Cliff faced the class. He asked, "Do you?"

● ● ●

At lunch, the kids talked about Father Cliff's lesson.

Riley said, "There's nothing like it."

"Like what?" Kim asked.

"Like bread and wine becoming the Body and Blood of Jesus," he replied.

"What are you talking about?" Brad asked.

Riley said, "I can't find any examples of it."

"What do you mean by 'examples'?" Sam asked. She hoped this wasn't another test for her and Nick. She glanced across at Nick. He was busy eating his peanut butter and jelly sandwich.

Riley opened his lunch bag. "You know, when we say that one thing is kind of like another?" he asked.

Brad groaned. "I don't know what you're talking about."

"Yes you do," Riley said. "I had a teacher who tried to tell us about the God the Father and Jesus the Son and the Holy Spirit being one, but being different, too. She said it is like water. Water can be a liquid and it can be steam and it can be ice. Three different things, but the same."

"You're talking about an *analogy*," Kim said.

"My dad used to drive an *analogy*," Brad joked. "It was a sporty car."

Riley wasn't put off. "I mean, there isn't anything else in the world like Jesus being in the bread and wine. All we can do is believe it."

"Like you believe in Big Foot?" Brad said.

Riley shook his head. "That's different. People have seen Big Foot. There are tracks and stuff. It might be out there somewhere. But it doesn't matter if it isn't real."

Sam was surprised to hear Riley say that.

"How is that different?" Brad asked.

Sam couldn't tell if Brad was being serious or just trying to argue. Maybe he was doing both.

"Believing in Communion matters," Riley said. "But we need to have faith to believe it."

"Faith is what they tell us to have when they can't explain things," Brad said.

Sam looked at Kim.

"You always say that," Kim said.

Brad looked at the girls like he was taking a dare. "It's true," he said.

The two girls rolled their eyes.

"I can't pretend like a wafer is somebody's flesh and wine is somebody's blood," Brad said.

"We're not supposed to pretend," said

Sam. "We're supposed to go past what they look and feel like. We're supposed to believe they're what Jesus said they are."

"That's faith," Kim said.

Brad hit his hand against the table. "See? You can't explain it, so you want me to have faith."

Kim growled at him. "You're so frustrating."

Nick had been eating quietly. Sam could tell he was thinking hard about what they were saying. He put down his sandwich and said, "Faith is like a promise."

All eyes turned to him.

"When your parents say you'll get something as a birthday present, you don't know how they'll get it or what kind of wrapping it'll have or where it came from, right?" he said.

"I guess," Brad said.

"You believe your parents because you trust them," Nick said. "You believe they'll give you the birthday present because they said so. That's faith."

Brad opened his mouth like he might say something funny, but then he closed it again.

"Have faith in Jesus or don't," Nick said. "Don't pretend."

Nick picked up his sandwich and started to eat again.

Sam gazed at her brother. *Sometimes I don't think I know him at all*, she thought.

"Big Foot *is* real, by the way," Riley said.

The girls moaned.

Chapter Eleven

——•——

Jars and Jolts

"Gather up your science project. We're going to Uncle Clark's," Mr. Perry called to Nick from the kitchen.

Sam perked up. It was early Saturday afternoon and she was sitting at the kitchen table doing her math homework. "You're going to the Old Perry House?"

Nick came in from the family room. He had been watching a TV program. "Why?" Nick asked.

Their father picked up his car keys.

"The yard is a lot bigger. We can test your paper airplanes. Remember? We need to see how far the different weights of paper will fly."

"I'll be right back," Nick said. He ran to the stairs.

"Can I go, too?" Sam asked.

"You'll have to," he said. "Your mom is volunteering at the soup kitchen. Andrew is at the library. Lizzy is at a birthday party. I won't leave you here alone."

Sam closed her math folder. She got up and went to find her shoes.

Ten minutes later they pulled into the long driveway that led to the Perry House. Mr. Perry stopped the car under the roof of what was once the carriage entrance.

Uncle Clark opened the large front door. He stepped out. He was taller and more muscular than their father. He had a shaved head that made his face look round. Today he was wearing a blue pullover, black jeans, and brown boots. He waved hello.

The family got out of the van.

Sam expected Jake, Uncle Clark's dog, to run up to them. The dog didn't appear. "Where's Jake?" she asked.

"He's up at the construction site. He likes it better up there," Uncle Clark said, then added, "So do I."

"We won't stay long," Sam's father said. He shook his brother's hand.

"Don't worry. I'm trying to get some work done, that's all." He waved for them to come in. "I have something to show you."

They stepped into the front hall. Uncle Clark closed the door. It made a loud *thump* and echoed throughout the massive house.

Sam looked around as if she'd never been in there before. The front hall had white tiled floors and a tall ceiling with an iron chandelier hanging down. A staircase with chocolate-colored banisters curled upstairs. The walls had dark wood panels with carvings shaped like diamonds.

There was a big room to the left that Sam once heard someone call a "reception room." Uncle Clark now used it as his office. One door over was a library with endless shelves and a big fireplace. Next to that was the dining room and the kitchen and small rooms for the servants who worked there years ago.

On the second floor were the master bedroom, five other bedrooms, and three more small rooms for the servants. The master bedroom led out to a balcony that looked like a round tower in a castle.

Nick and Sam and their family used to stay in the bedrooms when they came to visit. The kids used the old servants' rooms to play in.

The third floor had a room for a pool table and other types of games. There was a large guest bedroom next to that and rooms for storage.

Sam looked at Nick as they stood in the front hall. She knew he was thinking what she was thinking: *I wish we lived here.*

"Come on down to the basement," Uncle Clark said.

They followed him through the dining room to the pantry. It was a square room with shelves for food. Most of the shelves were empty or had old bottles and cans on them. There was a door on the far wall that opened to a set of stairs.

Uncle Clark turned on a light. They went down the stairs. The basement was the shape of the house above them. It had cement walls and an uneven floor. There was a massive furnace off to one side with pipes going this way and that.

Old metal cabinets lined another wall. A different wall had a big work table with tools hanging on the wall above it. Big boxes were stacked near yet another wall. Some of the boxes had tinsel sticking out of them and a fake Christmas tree leaning to one side.

"This way," Uncle Clark said. They went further back. He had to turn on more lights as they went. Finally, they came to a corner room with its own door and a window. The door had several locks on it. So did the window. The panes were frosted so no one could see in or out. The corner of one pane had a giant spider's web in it.

"I was clearing out this room and found *that*." Uncle Clark pointed to the windowsill. Lined up along the edge were six Mason jars with something inside each one.

"Is that what I think it is?" Sam's dad asked. He and the kids drew closer.

Inside the jars were a murky liquid and nails covered in a fuzzy kind of rust. Sam saw small cards with a kid's handwriting tucked under the bottom of each jar.

"It's your science project," Uncle Clark said proudly.

"It's still here," Sam's dad said in a whisper. "After 30 years."

His eyes were big. He had a big smile on his face. Sam thought he looked like a little boy.

Nick came in for a closer look. He

looked from one jar to the next.

Uncle Clark said, "I doubt anyone meant to keep it. We didn't come to this room very often. You must have put it here, and everyone forgot about it."

Nick read the cards out loud. "Tap water. Bottled water. Cola. Orange juice. Vinegar. Bleach."

Uncle Clark picked up a large piece of light green poster board from behind a box and a bicycle without wheels.

"That's my display," Mr. Perry said.

The poster board was light green with large black letters that said, "How Long Does It Take a Nail to Rust?" Beneath were handwritten paragraphs and pictures and graphs.

"You got a B-plus," Sam said. She pointed to the red handwriting in the upper right-hand corner.

"Sister Doris," her dad said. "No one got an A from Sister Doris unless you cured cancer."

"I wish I could hand this in," Nick said. "Everyone'll think it's so cool to have a project from *ancient* times."

"Watch it, kid," his dad said. He knelt closer to one of the jars. "The science teacher might think it's interesting."

"What should I do with this stuff?" Uncle Clark asked. "Throw it all away?"

"Why were you clearing this room?" Mr. Perry asked.

"It's long overdue," Uncle Clark said. "And I want it to look good for the real estate agent."

Sam saw her father tense up. "For the what?" he asked.

Uncle Clark put his hands on his hips. "We talked about this, Jon. It's time to sell this old place."

"You can't!" the three Perrys said at the same time.

Uncle Clark laughed.

"Why?" Nick asked.

"I'm hardly ever here," Uncle Clark

said. "It's too big for me anyway."

"I understand," Mr. Perry said. "But this house is part of our family."

"We've had this argument a dozen times," Uncle Clark said. "Do you want it?"

"Yes!" Sam and Nick shouted.

"Wait," their father said. "A house like this takes a lot of work—and money."

"My point exactly," Uncle Clark said. "I have a couple of buyers who want to turn it into a bed-and-breakfast. Or maybe divide it into apartments."

"That would wreck it," Sam said.

Uncle Clark put a hand on his brother's shoulder. "I need to make a decision in the next couple of weeks."

"We'll talk about it," Mr. Perry said.

Sam followed her dad and brother to the front hall again. Nick got the box with his science project from the van.

Her dad looked inside. "Did you *throw* everything in?" he asked Nick.

"We were in a rush," Nick said.

"But you crumpled some of the planes. They won't fly now," Mr. Perry told him.

Nick looked surprised.

"We'll have to make new ones," his father said. "Did you bring more paper?"

Nick knelt down. He took the plain paper out of the box. "Here."

Mr. Perry knelt down next to him. "Let's get to work."

Uncle Clark dropped to his knees. "All right if I help? I haven't made paper airplanes in *years*."

• • •

That evening, Sam wrote in her project diary:

2 hours. Built paper airplanes with Uncle Clark. Nick & Dad tested different paper weights and sizes in the yard. Pretended they were pilots

in World War II. Chased each other around the yard with the planes. Threw snowballs. 3 planes destroyed. Test results?

Brought Dad's nail project home. Mom was disgusted.

30 minutes. I am nervous about the tests on me and Nick.

CHAPTER TWELVE

—— • ——

Riley and Roses

It was Monday morning when Sister Lucy took Nick, Sam, and Riley aside and said, "I've cleared it with your parents. We'll do the science project tests after school today."

Riley was grinning at them. "I can't wait!"

"Today?" Sam asked. Her voice was a dry croak.

"I don't want to drag it out for you," Sister Lucy said. "I know you're anxious."

"Who said I'm anxious?" Sam said.

Sister Lucy laughed. She patted her on the arm.

"Are we supposed to do anything to get ready?" Nick asked.

"Just have a normal day," Sister Lucy said.

"*I'll* be able to do that," Nick said. He looked at his sister.

She looked wild-eyed.

"It'll be okay," Riley said.

Sam turned on him. "Easy for you to say. You're not the guinea pig."

"*Sam*," Sister Lucy said sharply.

"I'm sorry," Sam said. "I didn't mean that. I don't know why I'm so nervous."

Sister Lucy crouched down to face Sam. "Try to relax."

A little later, Nick whispered to her, "What's wrong with you? Are you scared they're going to learn that we have a weird twin connection?"

Sam twisted the bottom of her sweater. "Now I'm afraid they'll find out we don't."

Nick went bug-eyed. "That we *don't*? But I thought—"

"I know," Sam said with a frown. "But now I want kids like Brad to believe that mysteries like the Eucharist are possible."

Nick sighed deeply. "We may have a special bond, but I'll never figure you out," he said.

• • •

Nick went out for recess. He kept thinking about the tests later on, though he didn't want to think about them. He was about to join the other kids on the playground when he saw Mr. Norm standing at a small wooden table next to the work shed. Nick went over to see what he was doing.

Nick heard Mr. Norm humming to himself. He was putting soil in a dark red flower pot.

Nick stepped up. "Hi, Mr. Norm."

"Nick," he said. "I've been thinking."

Nick waited. He knew that when Mr. Norm said "I've been thinking" that he was thinking about something interesting in a good and a weird way.

"When's the last time God created anything really new?" Mr. Norm asked.

Nick was surprised. "You mean, 'new' like something that has never existed before?"

"Yeah," Mr. Norm said.

Nick thought about it. "He hasn't."

"Not since the Garden of Eden," Mr. Norm affirmed.

Nick waited again.

"God made man from dust." Mr. Norm held up his hands. His fingers were caked with the potting soil. "The Bible says that *first* he formed man from the dust of the ground."

Nick remembered that and said so.

Mr. Norm continued, "And then God breathed his Spirit into man. That's when man became a living soul."

Nick had no idea where Mr. Norm was going with this talk.

Mr. Norm shifted his toothpick to the other side of his mouth without touching it. "God took the dead dust he created and made something living out of it."

"Just like he took plain water and made it into wine," Nick said.

Mr. Norm gave a slow nod. "He also takes plain water and gives us spiritual life in Baptism."

"Uh huh," Nick said. He waited.

Mr. Norm returned to the soil and the pot. "God doesn't create brand-new things. He uses the ordinary things he's already created and breathes new life into them."

Mr. Norm was quiet for a long time.

Nick asked, "Is that what you were thinking about?"

Mr. Norm looked down at him. "I was *thinking*: if God can put his Spirit into dust and make man, then he can put his Spirit into anything."

Nick saw a connection to what Father Cliff had been teaching them. "Bread and wine?"

"Bread and wine," Mr. Norm said softly.

Nick thought of the question, *how small is God*?

Mr. Norm shifted from the pot and the soil to a small burlap bag. He carefully unwrapped it. Lying inside was a red rose on top of a small tangle of stems. Its roots spread wildly at the bottom.

Nick gasped. "Is that the rose Sister Lucy found by the fence?"

"The very one," Mr. Norm said. "I'm moving it so I won't mow it down." He carefully put the rose into the soil.

Nick watched him. "Will it live?"

"It survived the winter," Mr. Norm said with a gentle chuckle. "Let's pray it'll survive *my* care."

CHAPTER THIRTEEN

— • —

Tests and Turnouts

The bell rang for the school day to end. Nick, Sam, and Riley waited in their seats while the other students left.

Brad lingered a little, then said to Nick before he walked out, "I hope you don't mind electrodes."

Riley said quickly, "We're not using electrodes."

"What are electrodes?" Sam asked. Her sweater was all twisted up.

"He was joking," Nick said to her.

She looked worried.

"Ready?" Sister Lucy asked.

The kids stood up.

She said, "We're going to Mr. Noble's science lab. He's interested in this project. He also has two rooms we can use."

Mr. Noble welcomed the four them as they came through the door. "This is one of the most original science projects I think we've ever done here," he said.

"Wait until you see my dad's nail collection," Nick said.

"We helped Riley come up with some of the tests," Sister Lucy said. She gestured to Riley. "It's his project, so he has to take the lead."

"Oh yeah," he said. "Sister Lucy and I will take Sam into that room." He pointed to a room at the back of the lab. "Nick, you'll stay here with Mr. Noble."

"Then what?" Sam asked.

"We'll ask you some questions and do a couple of physical tests," Riley said.

"That's all."

"This way," Sister Lucy said. She guided Sam to the other room.

"I'll be right back," Riley said and followed them. He closed the door.

"Sit down, Nick," Mr. Noble said. He waved to a folding chair nearby.

Nick sat down. He looked at Mr. Noble. "Does science say anything about twins and their special sense?" he asked.

Mr. Noble gave a small tilt of his head, like a shrug. "Not much. There's a lot we don't know about the brain. It's hard for science to explain things like intuition or the things that go beyond our normal senses."

Nick looked at the closed door. "Should I be doing anything?"

"It's better if we don't talk right now," he said. He took a notepad out of his pocket and began to write something on it. "Just be still."

Nick waited. He tried to imagine

what was going on with Sam. He knew his parents wouldn't allow anything dangerous.

"Are you thinking of any colors right now?" Mr. Noble asked him.

"Colors? You mean, like my favorite?" Nick asked.

"No," he said. "Did any colors come to mind while you were sitting there?"

"No. But now I'm thinking of pink," Nick said.

"Is that your favorite color?" Mr. Noble asked.

Nick shook his head.

Mr. Noble made a note. "Anything else come to mind?"

"I just thought of a tractor," Nick said. He wasn't sure why. "The old one up at my uncle's construction site."

Mr. Noble made another note.

Nick thought he heard a muffled *bang* in the other room like someone had dropped something heavy.

"What are you thinking now?" Mr. Noble asked him.

"I thought of a book hitting the floor," Nick said.

"Hmm," Mr. Noble said. He scribbled some more.

They sat silently for another couple of minutes. Nick looked at the microscope. His mind wandered back to the question of *how small is God?* He thought about the rose in the snow. He wondered about the First Communion retreat next weekend.

Then the door opened.

Riley came out alone. He was carrying a clipboard.

"Where's Sam?" Nick asked.

"She's in with Sister Lucy," Riley said.

Nick looked at the closed door. "Is she all right?"

"Yeah. We have to keep her away from you for this part of the test," Riley said.

Nick sat up. "It's my turn?"

Riley walked over and stood next to Mr. Noble. "I'm going to ask you some questions really fast. Say whatever comes to mind."

"Okay," Nick said. "Go ahead.

"Think of a color," Riley said.

"Blue."

Mr. Noble asked, "Is that your favorite color?"

"Yes."

Riley said, "Think of any kind of bird."

"Pelican."

"Think of a something long and thin."

"Straw."

"Think of a four-legged animal."

"Dog."

"Think of a special place."

"Perry House."

"Think of a cartoon character."

"Bugs Bunny."

"Think of a kind of food."

"Lasagna."

"Think of a special person you know."

"Mr. Norm."

"Think of a piece of clothing."

"T-shirt."

"Think of something that holds water."

"Bucket."

"Now, stand up and stretch your arms as high as they'll go."

Nick stood up and put his arms up in the air.

"Higher," said Riley.

Nick pushed them higher.

"Higher."

Nick pushed them as high as he

could. His muscles burned.

"Now put your hands at your side and jump up and down as fast as you can."

Nick pressed his hands at his side and jumped up and down. "Like this?" he asked.

"Yeah. Straight up and down," Riley said.

Nick jumped up and down. He could feel his heart pounding faster. Then he felt silly and started to laugh.

"Sit down again," Riley said.

Nick did. Mr. Noble stood up. He went to the other side of the long table with the microscopes. He came back with a bowl. It had water in it. He held it out to Nick.

"Put your hands in that," Riley said.

Nick looked at the two of them. "Is it hot or cold?"

"Put your hands in," Riley said again.

Nick braced himself. He put his hands in the water. It was ice cold. "Yikes," he said.

Riley waited a few seconds. Then he said, "You can take them out."

Mr. Noble handed Nick a small towel.

"Thanks," Nick said. He dried his hands.

Mr. Noble went behind Nick.

"We're going to cover your eyes," Riley said.

Mr. Noble put a large cloth over his eyes. It felt like a cotton hood.

Nick waited. He could hear Riley moving around. "Am I supposed to do something?"

He felt something soft tickling his left cheek. It felt like a bug was crawling on his skin. He instinctively reached up to knock it away. Nothing was there.

"I hope this is part of the test," Nick said.

Something soft tickled his other cheek. He tried not to react this time. But the tickling kept on. Finally, he moved his hand to swat at it.

"That's good," Riley said.

"Keep the blindfold on," Mr. Noble told him.

A warm spray hit Nick's face. "Hey!" he said and shook his head.

"It's just water," Riley said. "Now I want you to tilt back in that chair as far as you can."

"Like this?" Nick said and used his legs to tilt the chair backward. He reached a point where he thought he might tip over and stopped.

Suddenly the chair felt like it had gone too far.

"Whoa!" Nick jerked forward to put the four legs down on the floor again. "What are you guys doing?"

"Relax," Riley said. "Mr. Noble was ready to catch you."

Nick reached up for the blindfold.

"Not yet," Riley said.

Nick frowned. He was ready for the test to end.

Bang!

The explosion came fast. Nick jumped. He grabbed the blindfold and tore it off.

Mr. Noble was standing next to a large book on the floor. "You were right before," he said with a smile. "Riley dropped a book in the other room."

Nick looked at Riley. "You did all this to Sam?"

Riley nodded. "Except I changed a couple of the questions."

"Shall we compare notes?" Mr. Noble said.

Riley went to the closed door. He pushed it open. Sam and Sister Lucy came into the lab. Sam looked calmer than she did coming in. Sister Lucy was carrying a clipboard.

"What happened?" Sam asked. She sat down at a desk near Nick.

"We're done being lab rats," Nick said, trying to make a joke.

Nobody laughed.

Riley, Mr. Noble, and Sister Lucy

huddled together. They whispered and pointed to their clipboards.

Nick and Sam shared a look.

Riley looked at the twins. He had an unhappy look on his face. "It didn't work," he said.

Mr. Noble and Sister Lucy sat down at two of the desks.

"What do you mean?" Nick asked.

"It worked," Mr. Noble said. "But the results aren't what Riley wanted."

"You didn't answer the questions the same," Riley said. "And you didn't *think* of the answers to the questions I was asking the other twin."

Nick turned to Mr. Noble. He said, "When you asked me if I was thinking about a color, Riley was asking Sam about a color?"

"That's right," he said.

"I thought of orange," Sam said.

"You said you were thinking of 'red,'" Mr. Noble said. "And you answered 'blue' to the question."

"I was probably thinking of red because of the rose I saw earlier," Nick said. Then he remembered thinking about a tractor. "Was that because you asked her about a vehicle?"

Riley frowned. "I didn't ask her about vehicles. I changed the question and asked her about a kind of jewel."

Sister Lucy looked down at her clipboard. "We tickled Sam's face with a feather," she said. "You didn't feel anything in here. When Riley tickled your face, Sam didn't feel anything."

Mr. Noble tapped his notepad. "Neither of you reacted to the cold water. We were sure that one of you might feel the cold sensation while the other's hands were in the bowl."

"What about the chair?" Sam asked. "It scared me when you tipped me back."

"Me, too," Nick said.

"But you didn't feel it," Riley said.

"He means, neither of you felt what the other was feeling," Mr. Noble said. "The same when you were startled by the dropped book."

Sam looked at Riley, then Mr. Noble and Sister Lucy. "We don't have a special bond?" she asked.

"All this means is that whatever happens between you as twins isn't proven by these tests," Mr. Noble said.

Nick gave a sympathetic look to Riley. "Sorry, Riley. Do you have to do another project?"

"No," said Sister Lucy. "The science project asked, 'Do twins have a special psychic connection?' The tests tried to answer the question. The results will go on his display."

"That's it?" Nick asked.

"That's it," said Riley. His frown had nearly turned into a pout.

• • •

"Why didn't any of the tests work?" Sam asked Nick later at home.

Nick had been asking himself the same question. He felt a little disappointed that the other kids wouldn't think he was some kind of superhero. "Are you upset?" he asked Sam.

"I'm confused," Sam said. "And Brad might not have faith now."

Nick sighed. "Brad will decide what he believes without us," he said. "I just think he likes to argue."

Sam gazed at him. "But one of the tests should have worked," she said.

"Maybe the twin thing doesn't work when we're trying to make it work," Nick said. "Maybe we can't force it like that."

Sam looked hopeful. "Really?"

"How am I supposed to know?" Nick asked. "I'm just a lab rat."

Sam's project diary entry:

45 minutes. Mom and Dad said our science projects are due on Monday. We have to do our displays before the First Communion retreat on Saturday, or there won't be enough time. Nick and I panicked.

CHAPTER FOURTEEN

———.———

Projects and Panics

The rest of the week was spent on the science project displays.

Sam wrote in her project diary . . .

Tuesday.

10 minutes. Dad nagging Nick to start on his display and Nick saying "I will" but then he got distracted by a TV program.

5 minutes. New nagging by Dad.

13 minutes. Nick looking for the paper airplane test results he had written down.

1 hour. Mom watched Nick copy test results to pieces of construction paper. Argued about the color of cardboard.

1 hour. Dad watched me copy parts of this journal onto construction paper for display.

Did not finish displays.

Wednesday.

1 hour. Dad and Nick pasted lettering on his poster board. Argued whether lettering should be straight on uneven. Nick sat on construction paper covered in paste. Had to rewrite results on the piece.

39 minutes. Mom and I did lettering on my poster board. Chose frilly letters. Lizzy gave me ideas about how to put construction paper on poster board.

Thursday.

2 hours. Dad, Mom, and Nick battled over the display. Nick wanted to add pictures of different planes he liked. Mom said it looked too cluttered. Dad let him do a couple of planes in the corners.

23 minutes. I finished my display except for the last panel.

Friday.

56 minutes. Nick finished his display.

20 minutes. Writing this last entry onto construction paper for display. Dad helped me write in the totals. Mom and Dad do not like telling the whole school about our stress.

Nick wishes he had done the project on nails. Wants to take Dad's old nail project into Mr. Noble.

Science projects ready to hand in.

CHAPTER FIFTEEN

— · —

Thoughts and Thankfulness

Saturday came. Mr. Perry took Nick and Sam to the First Communion retreat at St. Clare's. They met in one of the larger classrooms in the church. Father Cliff had set up a table at the front of the room. It had a small crucifix, a gold chalice and a gold bowl with a lid, and white napkins.

Sister Lucy and Sister Monica handed out folders as they came in. The two third-grade classes filled the folding

chairs. Sam saw kids that attended the church but didn't go to the school.

Nick saw Brad and Riley. He went off to sit with them.

Sam sat next to Kim. She opened the folder. It had pages with pictures of Jesus and his disciples seated at a table and paragraphs of Scripture and explanations of the Mass. There were also word puzzles and fill-in-the-blank questions.

Sister Lucy called out for everyone to bow their heads. They did the Sign of the Cross and prayed. Then Father Cliff stepped out from behind the table.

"Today we're going to get ready for your First Communion," he said. "To do that, we'll go back to one of the greatest events in history. The very first Mass."

He told them to open their folders to the picture of Jesus at the table with his disciples. "Jesus was celebrating the Passover feast with his disciples.

You've learned about the Passover feast in class, right?"

Most of the kids said they had. Sam remembered that it was a feast from the Old Testament. The Israelites ate a meal to remember that God has saved them from death and freed them from the Egyptians.

Father Cliff drifted back behind the table. "Jesus sat at a table with his disciples. Does this look familiar? You see it at every Mass. The priest is at the altar, and he holds up the bread and tells the story of how on the night Jesus was betrayed, he took bread and, giving thanks, said the blessing, broke the bread, and gave it to his disciples. Jesus said, 'Take this, all of you, and eat of it, for this is my Body which will be given up for you.'" He held up the wafer. "Does everyone remember those words?"

Many of the kids nodded.

He put down the wafer and picked up the gold chalice. It glittered in the light. "Then the priest holds up the chalice. He reminds us that Jesus took the chalice of wine that night and, after giving thanks, gave it to his disciples. He said, 'Take this, all of you, and drink from it, for this is the chalice of my Blood, the Blood of the new and eternal covenant, which will be poured out for you and for many for the forgiveness of sins. Do this in memory of me.'"

He put the chalice down again. "It was a great scene of love, done the night before Jesus did his greatest Act of Love."

He gestured to the class. "Do you remember the Passover meal?"

Kim raised her hand. She said, "God told the nation of Israel to eat and drink so that death would pass over them."

"Thank you," Father Cliff said. "And the Passover meal had an unblemished lamb. It was a sacrifice for the people's sins. *Jesus* became that lamb. He sacrificed himself. That's why we say the words in the Mass, 'Lamb of God, you take away the sins of the world. Have mercy on us.'"

Sam thought about all the connections between the stories in the Bible. It was like they all came together with Jesus.

"Now think back to the Gospel of Saint John, chapter 6," Father Cliff said. "Remember when Jesus said that we must eat his flesh and drink his blood to have eternal life? Do you see what Jesus is doing at the Last Supper? He's offering every ounce of himself for us. Not as some kind of symbol, but as a very real offering—his Body is broken for us, his Blood is shed for us." He paused to scan the room. "Where did he break his body and shed his blood?"

One of the kids Sam didn't know raised his hand. "On the Cross," the boy said.

Father Cliff turned the crucifix around to face the children. Sam gazed at the figure of Jesus hanging on the Cross.

"Jesus allowed himself to be betrayed by one of his followers," Father Cliff said. "He was arrested as a criminal by the religious leaders in Jerusalem. They put him in chains and beat him and spit on him and made fun of him. Then they handed him over to the Roman rulers, who did the same thing to him. They nailed him to the Cross and hung him up so they could laugh at him. God was nailed to the Cross."

Sam looked at the pointy crown of thorns on Jesus's head and the nails in his hands and feet. *Jesus let men do this to him, for me,* she thought.

Father Cliff came around the table and looked at the crucifix. "Jesus did it because he loves us. And he did it because God asked him to do it. Jesus did what Adam and Eve failed to do in the Garden. He was the New Adam who obeyed. The death they brought into the world by eating the fruit from the forbidden tree was about to be defeated by Jesus."

Sam hadn't thought about Jesus and Adam and Eve. They disobeyed. Jesus obeyed. Even though it killed him.

Father Cliff turned to the kids. "And that was the biggest surprise to everyone. Jesus died and then came back from the dead! He *beat* death. We get to share in eternal life because he died and lived again."

He slowly circled around the altar. "Maybe you're thinking, 'We just heard all this at Easter. We know about it.'" He held up the wafer and chalice again. "Maybe you're wondering what a wafer and wine have to do with the Cross and rising from the dead?"

He paused to let the kids think about the question.

Then he said, "Jesus loves us. He said he would never abandon us or forsake us. So he did make provisions for us. Do you know what I mean by 'provisions'? It's like when your parents go out for an evening. They don't leave you to fend for yourselves. They bring in someone to stay with you. They make sure there is food and a roof over your head and warm beds. Jesus gave us his Holy Spirit and the Church to guide and protect us. And he gave us the sacraments to help us grow in our love for him."

"There's Baptism that washes us with water on the outside and cleans us spiritually on the inside," he said. "And there's the bread and wine. He told us that it becomes his Body and Blood. He puts himself *into* the bread and wine so we can put him *into* us. He becomes part of us by eating and drinking. Why? Because what we eat and drink really become part of us. Eat pizza, drink juice, take medicine—they become part of you and work through your bodies, right?"

A few of the kids nodded.

Father Cliff moved around to the edge of the folding chairs. "It's tough, I know. A small, dry, tasteless wafer. A swallow of wine. It's hard to think of them as the Body and Blood of Jesus. It's more than we can figure out. It looks like a wafer—it looks like wine— and that's all you'd see if you put them under a microscope. But it's *Jesus*. Because he loves us and wants us to be in him and for him to be in us."

He paused and waved to Sister Lucy and Sister Monica. "Now, we're going to break into small groups. You'll go over some of the papers in the folder together with Sister Lucy and Sister Monica. Deacon Chuck will come in to help. There are questions for you to fill out and puzzles for you to do."

He stepped aside and let Sister Lucy lead the class.

. . .

During the next part of the class, Deacon Chuck went to a chalkboard that sat on wheels. He wrote in large letters *Eucharisteo.* He said slowly, "You-kar-is-toe."

Deacon Chuck underlined the word. "Do you know why we call it the Eucharist?" he asked.

No one answered.

"It's a big Greek word that means 'give thanks.'" Deacon Chuck tapped the board with the chalk. "The Mass is a time for us to give thanks. It's not about 'what am I getting out of this?' or 'am I having a good time?' It's about giving thanks for the gift that God has given us in his Son."

Father Cliff came alongside Deacon Chuck.

"Maybe you still don't get it," Father Cliff said. "That's all right. There are times in our lives when we have to accept things by faith. Your parents take you to the doctor to get a shot to keep you from getting a disease. Nobody explains the exact chemical formula in the needle. You don't feel sick and you don't know what disease they're talking about. But you do it because you trust them."

Sam remembered the talk they had at lunch about trust.

Father Cliff went on. "If Sister Lucy

or Sister Monica started telling you about quantum physics, you'd be right to say 'Wait a minute, I'm in third grade! How am I supposed to understand that when I have a hard time multiplying numbers?'"

Some of the kids laughed.

Father Cliff smiled at them. "Jesus knows that some things are hard for us to understand. We can't know everything God knows. So he asks us to trust him. Trust his Church. Don't wrack your brain trying to understand for now. Try to accept the beauty and the mystery by faith."

Father Cliff nodded to Deacon Chuck.

Deacon Chuck said, "Now let's practice what happens when you go up to receive Communion."

The class practiced getting in line and how to take the wafer and how to drink from the chalice. Sam felt funny opening her mouth for the wafer to be put on her tongue. She worried that she might drop the chalice.

After the rehearsal, Father Cliff announced that he would hear their confessions the next Friday after the school's morning assembly. "Then you'll be ready to take your First Communion at Sunday Mass," he said. "I'm very excited for you."

The next morning at Mass, Sam watched carefully. She listened to the words like never before. She could imagine Jesus with the disciples at the Last Supper. She observed how the people took the wafer and held the chalice. Some knelt. Some held out their hands. Some kept their hands folded in prayer. Some did the Sign of the Cross as they stepped away.

How will I feel? she wondered.

Chapter Sixteen

—·—

Displays and Disappearances

On Monday morning the Perry family left extra time to get Nick's and Sam's science project displays into the van. Sam's display seemed easy compared to Nick's. Nick carried an extra box with the different paper airplanes in it. He wanted to set them on the table for the kids to see.

Meanwhile, Nick's dad took his jars of rusty nails to Mr. Noble in the lab. Nick was happy to see Mr. Noble's reaction. The science teacher looked like he had just been given a special present.

Sister Lucy set up tables around the classroom so the displays could be set up first thing. "We'll put up the displays now, but we'll talk about them after recess," she said.

Nick sat down but looked at the different displays. He saw Brad's display about moldy Twinkle Cakes. Kim had done her project about the different kinds of water on plants. Sam's display about the impact of science projects made some of the kids laugh. There was a display about the solar system and one about the effect of the sun on hair growth and another on kittens and another on reptiles. It looked like everyone in the class had worked hard. But Riley wasn't there.

Nick wondered if Riley was sick with something, but then he came rushing in just as Sister Lucy was about to begin the class. He muttered an "I'm sorry" and struggled to keep from dropping his backpack and the big poster board. Sister Lucy helped him.

Riley's display was made mostly with construction paper and black magic marker. Everything was written in Riley's scrawl. Nick assumed Riley's father couldn't afford special lettering or fancy poster board. The headline at the top of the display asked, *DO TWINS HAVE SPECIAL POWERS?*

Nick couldn't read what Riley had written. He looked over at Sam. She was straining to see. Then she looked at Nick and shrugged.

Riley sat down at his desk on the other side of Sam. He didn't look very happy. "I should have done Big Foot," he said with a frown.

. . .

Riley grumbled a lot at lunch. "I don't like my project," he said. "I wanted to show that you *do* have special powers."

Nick wasn't sure whether he felt relieved or disappointed.

"I'll bet you wish you did my project about Twinkle Cakes," Brad said. "I never thought food could look so disgusting."

"Twinkle Cakes aren't food," Riley said sourly.

Brad laughed at him. "Don't be in such a bad mood. At least you got the project done. That's the point."

Riley scowled at him. He said to Nick, "I don't care what anyone says. You and Sam have something going on. You *know* things."

Nick didn't want him to start talking about it all again. "Maybe one day you'll find proof."

At the end of lunch, Brad said to Nick, "You have your airplanes hidden in that box. I want to see them. Bring them out to recess. We can see them fly."

"You can look at them," Nick said. "I want to keep them safe until we do our displays for the class."

"Bring them out to recess," Brad said.

Nick didn't see any harm in doing that. "Okay," he said.

It was another sunny day when the boys went out to the playground. A gentle breeze tickled the leaves of the trees. Nick carried the box to one of the picnic tables and took off the lid. Brad and Riley gathered around.

"Cool," Riley said.

"Which one flies the fastest?" Brad asked.

Nick picked up the one he called his F-16. He made it out of a sturdy gray construction paper.

Brad reached out. "Let's see," he said.

Nick handed it to him.

Brad held it by the long section under the wings. He smiled and said, "Let's try it."

"Don't," said Nick. "I don't want any-thing to happen to it."

Brad shook his head. "Just one time. Nothing will happen."

Before Nick could say anything, Brad jumped onto the picnic table bench and threw the paper airplane toward the playground.

"Brad!" Nick shouted.

The plane flew at an angle upward like an arrow shot from a bow. Nick was afraid it would land under someone's feet and get trampled. It curved like it might head for the ground, but a breeze grabbed it. The plane lurched and then floated higher.

"Look at it go!" Brad yelled.

Nick's eyes grew wide as the plane glided toward a tree. He feared it would get stuck in the branches. But then it gently turned. *It's coming back*, Nick thought and ran to catch it. Suddenly a gust of wind caught it. The plane shot up again and headed toward the school. Nick was sure it would slam into the brick wall. Then, at the last minute, the plane tilted up.

It didn't hit the wall but disappeared over edge of the school roof!

"No!" Nick cried out.

"Uh oh," Riley said.

Brad's face went pale. "How did that happen?" he asked in a shaky voice. "I didn't mean for that to happen."

"I told you not to throw it!" Nick said. "What am I supposed to do?"

• • •

Sister Lucy gave Nick a hall pass to go to the office. "Mr. Norm will have to go on the roof and get it," she said.

Sister Stephanie, the principal, was at the counter in the office when Nick walked in. He told her what had happened.

"I'm sorry, but Mr. Norm is at a dentist appointment," she said. "He'll be back in half an hour. I'll have him look for your plane then."

"Thank you," Nick said. He went back to class.

Sister Lucy said it was time for the class to show their projects. "We'll do them alphabetically. You can do yours last," she said to Nick.

Nick watched the clock while the other students presented their projects. He hardly listened. A half hour went by. No, Mr. Norm. Then an hour.

Did they forget? he worried.

Finally, Sister Lucy gave Nick another hall pass. "You can go to the office to ask about your plane," she said.

Nick leaped from his seat. He walked as fast as he could to the office. Just as he reached the door, he saw Mr. Norm walking away down another hall. Mr. Norm turned a corner and was out of sight.

Nick assumed he was going to get his plane from the roof. He ran after him.

St. Clare's wasn't a large school, but Nick didn't know the middle school wing very well. He passed various classes, including the science lab. Mr. Norm stayed far ahead.

Music now echoed down the hall. *This must be the band room*, Nick thought. There was a long hall that had one door in the middle. The music boomed loudly from behind the door.

Nick looked ahead. At the far end of the hall, Mr. Norm was working a key in a lock that was set high up on the door.

"Mr. Norm!" Nick called out.

Mr. Norm didn't hear him. He pulled open the door and stepped through.

Nick raced to the door. Mr. Norm had left it slightly ajar. Nick peeked in to see a short corridor and stairs going up. He thought he heard footsteps up at the top. He took a few steps into the passage. Cool air touched his face. He went to the bottom of the stairs and looked up.

"Mr. Norm?" he called out.

The air moved. The door slammed behind him.

The noise made Nick jump. A light flickered over his head. He looked at the door, then the stairs. He decided to go up the stairs.

He thought, *If it goes to the roof, then I can help Mr. Norm find my plane.*

Nick climbed the stairs. There were a lot of them. He felt breathless by the time he got to the top.

The stairs led to a small square room. It was empty. Over to the side, a ladder hung on the wall. Nick went to the bottom of the ladder and looked up. Clear skies were framed by the square of the hatch above him. Its metal door wobbled in the wind at the top.

Nick grabbed the bottom step of the ladder and started up.

The air became cooler and the draft

more constant as Nick climbed. Clutching two handles at the top, he pulled himself through.

He'd never seen the school roof before. It was covered with tar and gravel. Large square metal boxes with fans and vents were scattered here and there. Small pipes sat low and stretched out in different directions.

Nick saw Mr. Norm walking near the left side.

"Mr. Norm!" he shouted. He stepped onto the roof.

Mr. Norm looked up, surprised. "Stay back!" he called out. "Don't move from there!"

Nick saw something move on the gravel a few feet behind Mr. Norm. "My plane!" he shouted and pointed.

Mr. Norm glanced around, saw the plane and bent to pick it up. As he stooped down, a gust of wind caught the plane. It tumbled away. Mr. Norm

chased after it. The breeze kept the plane rolling just beyond his reach. He began to laugh.

Finally, with a lunge, he caught it. He straightened and held it up for Nick to see. "This must be it," he said.

He took a couple of steps in Nick's direction. "You did a good job on it," Mr. Norm said, turning the plane over in his hand.

Nick saw what Mr. Norm didn't see. A length of pipe was just in front of his feet. His left foot caught on it. He turned slightly and his right foot came down onto the pipe at a funny angle. He twisted and flew, hitting the rooftop with a crunchy thump.

Nick couldn't stay back. He ran over to the fallen man. "Are you all right?" he asked.

Mr. Norm rolled onto his back. He was laughing. "That was clumsy," he said. He was still clutching Nick's plane. "I hope I didn't hurt it," he said and handed it over.

The wings were slightly bent. "It's okay," Nick said.

Mr. Norm sat up. "I think I twisted my ankle."

Nick saw Mr. Norm's left boot lift a little.

"That hurts," he said. He turned onto his knees and tried to stand up. He winced. "Ouch." He sat down again.

"Can I help?" Nick asked.

"Only if you were a couple times bigger or I was a couple times smaller," he said. "I'll call the office."

He reached into a pocket in his overalls and pulled out a cell phone.

Nick could tell that something was wrong. The screen was cracked. Part of the back hung loose.

"I fell on it," Mr. Norm said. "You'll have to go down to the office for help."

"Okay," Nick said. A gust of wind hit him. He felt like it might knock him over.

"Careful," Mr. Norm said.

Nick steadied himself and headed for the hatch. "I'll be right back."

"Don't run. Watch that ladder," Mr. Norm said.

Nick reached the hatch and turned around to climb down the ladder. Another gust of wind pushed him in. He held tight to the handles and then the rungs as he lowered himself in.

He was halfway down the ladder when

the wind blew hard above him. He looked up. There was a loud wrenching sound and then the lid to the hatch came crashing down. Nick ducked as if the cover might fall on him. When it didn't, he climbed up to the top again. He took hold of the latch to the lid and tried to make it turn. It wouldn't budge. He pushed up on the cover. No luck.

Someone in the office will figure it out, Nick thought. He went back down the ladder. A dim yellow light helped him down the stairs. He could hear the band practicing down the hall. He came to the door and pushed. It was locked tight.

"Oh, come on," Nick whispered. He turned the door handle. It moved, but the door was still held fast. "What's wrong with this thing?"

He stepped back and looked. There was a lock further up. It was like a small box with a nob on it. He remembered that kind of lock from the old Perry

House. It locked by itself if the door closed. You had to turn the nob to unlock it again.

He reached up. The nob was beyond his fingertips. He got onto his tippy-toes. His fingers still didn't reach. He jumped as high as he could. His fingers brushed the nob, but he couldn't get a proper hold to turn it.

He looked around for something to stand on. Nothing.

He pounded on the door and yelled.

The band played loudly on the other side. He imagined the long empty hall with no other classrooms on it. *No one can hear me until the band stops playing,* he thought.

He turned to the stairs. With a sinking feeling, he realized he couldn't get back on the roof. Now he couldn't get through the door.

A whimper caught in his throat.

I'm trapped.

CHAPTER SEVENTEEN

———•———

Bonds and Belief

Sam watched her classmates talk about their displays. She felt a little nervous because her turn was coming up. She looked over at Nick's desk. She'd heard about the plane flying onto the roof. She knew he had gone to find Mr. Norm.

What was taking him so long? she wondered.

She felt something in her stomach. It was like a flutter with a slight sick feeling.

I'm nervous about my display, she thought. But she knew it was more than that. It was the same feeling she got when something was wrong with Nick.

She looked around for Sister Lucy.

Riley caught her eye. He saw her expression. His eyes went wide.

Sister Lucy was leaning against the wall by the window. She was watching Brandon give his presentation about how a light bulb works.

Sam approached her. "May I have a hall pass?" she asked.

"What's wrong?" Sister Lucy asked.

"Nick," she said. "He should be back by now. May I go find him?"

Sister Lucy went to her desk for a hall pass. "I don't want you to search for him. Go to the office."

"Yes, Sister," Sam said.

Sam did a half-walk/half-run to the office.

Sister Catherine was at the counter when Sam came in. Sam explained about

Nick and Mr. Norm and the airplane on the roof.

"I'll call Mr. Norm," Sister Catherine said and picked up her phone. She punched the buttons and listened. "It's going to his voicemail."

Sister Catherine stood up. "Wait here," she said. She went into Sister Stephanie's office.

Sam went back out into the hall. She didn't know why, but she had a feeling that Nick was in the middle school wing somewhere. The words "band practice" kept coming to her mind. She started down the hall.

"Sam," Sister Stephanie said behind her.

"He's this way," Sam said. She picked up her pace.

"Slow down," Sister Stephanie said.

But Sam was already running. She turned a corner and kept on. Sister Stephanie's footsteps echoed behind her. The sound of the band practicing was just ahead.

A hand fell on her shoulder. "Stop," Sister Stephanie said.

"But he's here somewhere," Sam said.

There was a thumping sound that didn't fit with the beat of the band's music.

Sister Stephanie said, "The stairs to the roof are there."

Sam and Sister Stephanie ran down the hall. The pounding grew louder.

"We're coming!" Sam shouted. She came to the door and pounded back. "Nick?"

Nick's voice was muffled on the other side.

Sister Stephanie pulled a set of keys from her pocket. She worked to find the right one and then pushed it into the lock. It clicked. She pulled the door open by the handle.

Nick was there. His face was smeared with lines of tears he'd been wiping away.

"Mr. Norm hurt his ankle. He's stuck on the roof," he said with loud sniffles.

"You two run to the office and tell Sister Catherine," Sister Stephanie said. "Hurry."

Sister Stephanie dashed through the doorway.

Sam took Nick's hand. They ran to the office.

• • •

Sam found out later that it took Father Cliff and Deacon Chuck to force open the lid to the hatch.

Sister Anne, the school nurse, wrapped Mr. Norm's ankle. Then Father Cliff and Deacon Chuck helped him down from the roof. Father Cliff drove him to the doctor for X-rays.

Sam talked about her project display. She told them about the many ways science projects caused stress at home. The kids laughed at some of her examples.

Sister Lucy asked her, "Do you think schools shouldn't require students to do science projects? Or even homework? Or is it possible that families need help to keep from stressing out?"

Sam thought about it and said, "I think stress is part of life, no matter what we do. We all need to learn how to cope with stress better."

"Good answer," Sister Lucy said.

Nick had calmed down enough to talk about his display, too. He glared at Brad the whole time he spoke.

Brad looked more ashamed than Sam had ever seen before.

Nick handed out his paper airplanes for the class to see, but Sister Lucy forbad anyone from flying them.

Riley stood up. He presented his display. He explained how he had done his tests on "two unnamed twins."

Everyone looked at Nick and Sam.

Riley told them that the tests couldn't prove that twins have a special sense about each other. "But I think they do. Something happened today to prove it."

Sister Lucy interrupted him. "Riley. If it's not part of your tests for the project, then you can't talk about it here."

"Aw," Riley said. He sat down. "You know it's true," he whispered to Sam.

Sam didn't respond.

• • •

That night the Perrys gathered in the family room after dinner. They took their usual spots on the couch, the chairs, and the floor. They talked about what had happened to Nick in the afternoon.

"You must have been scared," Lizzy said to her brother.

"I wasn't scared," Nick replied. "I was angry that I couldn't reach the lock."

"They put the locks up high so the students couldn't mess with them," Mr. Perry explained. "I'm sure they hadn't thought about kids going into that stairwell without a grown-up."

"I hope Mr. Norm is all right," Sam said.

"Sister Lucy said the X-rays were fine," Mrs. Perry told them. "He twisted his ankle like he thought. He'll have to use crutches for a while."

Nick asked Sam, "Did you really have a funny feeling about me?"

Sam nodded. "Now it's driving Riley crazy. He's going to nag us more than ever."

Andrew chuckled. "He'll get distracted

by something else. Alien kidnappings or the Goat Man of Jackson Lake."

"There's a Goat Man at Jackson Lake?" Nick asked.

"Stop it," Mrs. Perry said. "We're not talking about that."

"Pine Creek, not Jackson Lake," Mr. Perry corrected him in a low voice.

"*Stop*!" said Mrs. Perry.

Mr. Perry smiled at her.

Lizzy looked at Nick and said, "I hope Brad was sorry for what he did."

Nick grunted. "At first he tried to act like it was my fault. Then I reminded him that he has to go to Confession on Friday. That's when he said he was sorry."

"Good," Mr. Perry said.

Nick added, "He said he thought the way Sam found me was amazing. He told me he's going to think more about things like faith and mystery from now on."

Sam brightened up. "Really?"

"He'll still argue," Nick said. "He

always does."

"And now," Mr. Perry leaned forward on the couch and rested his hands on his knees. He said very seriously, "We have to talk about your First Communion."

Nick and Sam looked at each other.

"What do we have to talk about?" Sam asked. She looked worried.

"The Church expects us, as your parents, to state that you're ready for it," Mrs. Perry told them. "Are you ready?"

"What do you mean by 'ready'?" Nick asked.

Mr. Perry explained, "The Church wants to know that you accept the bread and wine as the Body and Blood of Jesus. You don't have to understand it all. But you have to give assent that you really believe what the Church teaches about it. You have to tell us you're okay to take it as a mystery."

"Well . . ." Nick started to say. "Yeah. I do."

"It's what Jesus said," Sam added. "So I believe it."

Their parents relaxed. So did Nick and Sam.

"One more thing," Mr. Perry said. "Uncle Clark invited us over to the house after your First Communion Mass. He wants to throw you a little celebration."

"Great!" Nick said. "Maybe we'll find more science experiments."

Mr. Perry laughed. "He did one with some dead frogs. Maybe they're still in his closet."

"*Ew!*" said the family.

Chapter Eighteen

——— • ———

Firsts and Family

The morning for the First Communion Mass was sunny and warm. It felt to Nick like springtime, like Easter Sunday should always be.

He wore a white shirt and dark blue tie, a black suit coat with matching pants, and dress shoes. The shoes pinched his feet a little, but he didn't mind.

Sam wore a long white dress and the white veil Lizzy wore for her First Communion. She looked nervous.

In the family van, Nick thought he

heard Sam whisper as a prayer, "Please, please, please don't let me drop the chalice."

Lizzy nudged Nick and whispered from the far back seat. "Sign this," she said.

He looked down. She handed him a folded piece of paper and a pencil.

He opened the paper. It was a drawing by Lizzy of his mother. Underneath it said, "Happy Mother's Day."

Nick put a hand over his mouth. He had forgotten it was Mother's Day because of everything else that had been going on.

Lizzy, Andrew, and Sam had already signed the card. He scribbled his name under theirs.

"I'll give it to her later," Lizzy said as Nick gave the drawing back to her.

The Mass had a lot more people than usual. Extra chairs were placed in the back. The families of the first communicants were given special places up front. Nick saw Brad and his family, Riley and his dad, and Uncle Clark, who gave him a small wave when they made eye contact. Mr. Norm stood off to the side with his crutches. He gave Nick a gentle salute.

The Mass began with Father Cliff welcoming everyone. He talked for a moment about the joy they all have in sharing this First Communion together with the children. Then the organ played and the choir sang.

Nick noticed that Father Cliff led the congregation in the renewal of baptismal vows instead of the Creed. After the Gospel reading, the priest talked about the great mysteries within our faith.

"That's one of the reasons I love being Catholic," he said. "We embrace an energetic and thoughtful theology along with the beauty of mystery."

He ended the homily by reading out

the names of everyone receiving their First Communion. He told them to stand up. "You will receive the Body and Blood first."

The Mass continued as it always did. Then came the time to stand and go forward to receive Communion.

Sam reached out and squeezed Nick's hand. "Pray I don't make a mistake," she said.

"You'll be fine," he whispered.

She went ahead of Nick.

He watched what she did, just to make sure he did it right. She didn't drop the chalice.

Nick stepped up to Father Cliff. The priest held up the wafer and said, "The Body of Christ."

Nick bowed. "Amen," he said.

Father Cliff put the wafer in his mouth.

It was flat and dry, but that didn't seem to matter very much.

Nick moved over to the chalice-bearer.

It was Sister Lucy. She smiled and said, "The Blood of Christ."

Nick gave a slight bow and said, "Amen."

She handed him the chalice.

It was heavier than he expected. *No wonder Sam was worried,* he thought. He took a small sip. The wine tasted sweeter than he expected. It was warm as it went down his throat.

He thought about what Father Cliff said. *Eating and drinking make something part of us.* He thought of the mystery of Jesus being in the wafer and wine, and now inside of him.

Nick took a few steps. He stopped to face the altar. He did the Sign of the Cross.

His eyes went to the large bouquet of flowers that adorned the long marble top. Then he caught sight of a small dark red pot that sat at the far edge.

A single rose sprung up proudly from it.

As he went back to the pew, Nick looked at the congregation. Mr. Norm stood in the back with his crutches. He gave Nick a modest salute.

Nick smiled at him.

• • •

Mass ended with Father Cliff offering a special prayer for all the mothers. Then there were hugs all around after they were dismissed.

Sam ran over to Kim to talk about their dresses.

Nick found Brad and Riley. Brad looked uncomfortable in his suit. He tugged at the collar.

Somehow Riley made his nice clothes look like he'd worn them to bed. But Riley was smiling.

"He was really there," Riley said.

Nick lifted an eyebrow. He asked, just to be sure, "Who was?"

"Jesus," Riley told him. "His presence."

"You could feel it?" Nick asked. He hadn't felt anything in particular. But he didn't think feelings were a big deal.

Riley shook his head. "I can't explain it," he said.

"I hope you two aren't going to get weird about it," Brad said.

"Weird?" Nick asked. "Who's weird?"

Not long after, the Perry family got into the van. Nick buckled his seatbelt.

"We're very happy for you," his father said from the front seat. "This is just the beginning of your journey of faith."

Sam sat next to Nick. She was grinning.

"What?" he asked.

"It's a world of mystery," she said for no reason he could think of.

A few minutes later they pulled into the driveway of the Old Perry House. Everyone leaped out and walked to the door.

Nick could hear Jake inside barking. Then Uncle Clark opened the door. Jake bounded out with barks and whines of excitement.

The kids took turns hugging and rubbing his fur.

"Easy, Jake. You don't want to ruin their clothes," Uncle Clark said.

Jake scampered away.

Uncle Clark led them to the dining room with its massive table. It was set up with plates of sandwiches cut into little squares. Bowls of pretzels and potato chips sat nearby.

A banner hung along one wall that said, "Blessings for the First Time!"

Underneath hung a poster with the handwritten words, "And Happy Mother's Day!"

The family nibbled on the sandwiches and chips for a little while. Uncle Clark then had the family sit down. He prayed for all of them to be drawn closer to God's love and the truth of his Church.

Nick peeked over at his father, who

often prayed the same prayer. *That must be a Perry family tradition,* he thought.

As soon as the prayer was finished, a man and a woman dressed in black-and-white servants' uniforms came through the kitchen door. They carried trays of hot meat and vegetables that they served to each of them.

Nick wondered if that's how it was years ago when the house was first built. Lizzy presented her homemade Mother's Day card to their mom. Mrs. Perry smiled and thanked them. Then their father gave her a half-dozen roses. "You deserve more for being the best mother a family could wish to have," he said.

She went around the table and hugged them all one by one.

After the meal, Uncle Clark looked at his brother and said, "Well? Isn't it time?"

Mr. Perry gave him a coy smile.

"Time for what?" Andrew asked.

"We have a decision to make," his father replied. "Uncle Clark wants to move out of this house. Your mother and I want to move in. But we won't do it unless you all agree. What do you think?"

With one voice, the Perry children shouted out, "We agree!"

And Nick knew that another adventure was about to happen.

Read *MORE* Adventures of Nick & Sam!

Learn more at
AugustineInstitute.org/books